TRIGGER POINT

GIACOMO GIAMMATTEO

Inferno Publishing Company

© Copyright **2025** Giacomo Giammatteo

All rights reserved. No part of this book may be reproduced or transmitted in any form or by any means, electronic or mechanical, including photocopying, recording, or by any information storage and retrieval system, without written permission from the author, except for the inclusion of brief quotations in a review.

This ebook is licensed for your personal enjoyment only. This ebook may not be resold or given away to other people. If you would like to share this book with another person, please purchase an additional copy for each reader. If you're reading this book and did not purchase it, or it was not purchased for your use only, then please return to

INFERNO PUBLISHING COMPANY, Houston, Texas.

For more information about this book, visit Giacomo's website.

Book design by Giacomo Giammatteo

This edition was prepared by Giacomo Giammatteo gg@giacomog.com

Print ISBN 978-1-949074-81-9

Electronic ISBN 978-1-949074-80-2

This book is a work of fiction. Names, characters, places, and events herein are either the product of the author's imagination or are used fictitiously. Any resemblance to actual persons, living or dead, is entirely coincidental.

❀ Formatted with Vellum

Chapter One
KAFEH SUPREME - DAMASCUS

Year 2044

Kafeh Supreme, once elegant, now bore the scars of years of conflict — wars that didn't have to happen. Sunlight filtered through bullet-riddled walls, and the floor was covered with cracked floor tiles, dirt filling the spaces between them.

Cyrus sat at a corner table, positioned so he could see both the front and back exits. He scanned the cafe with haunted eyes that rarely blinked while he tapped the tabletop with restless fingers, and occasionally sipped from his cup of espresso.

He cradled his coffee cup, inhaling the aroma that wafted through the café. All his life he'd smelled the unmistakable aroma of espresso, and his morning breakfast always had a steaming cup of it, even when he was in elementary school.

Customers soon filled the café, and it buzzed with hushed conversations, but the locals avoided eye contact with strangers. They kept to themselves and spoke in whispers.

Cyrus looked over when the door opened, letting in a blast of dusty air, a lingering hint of gunpowder riding in with it. Sandof walked through the door, a jagged scar tracing from ear to collarbone. One eye was slightly askew, but he scanned the room with practiced caution.

As he walked across the café, Shaklam entered, his fingers drumming against his thigh. His eyes darted left and right at every sound. He moved with the nervous energy of youth.

Rizwan followed Shaklam, and he carried himself with exaggerated confidence. He paused halfway through and lifted his head, and inhaled deeply, then made his way to Cyrus's table.

"I never tire of the smell of good espresso. It reminds me of my grandmother's house before the war."

"Keep those memories," Cyrus said. "You'll need them."

A waiter, his shoulders permanently hunched, and his eyes downcast, arrived to take orders. He appeared to be not paying attention, but he missed nothing. He held a notepad clutched like a shield.

"Your orders, gentlemen?"

Rizwan spoke first. He had the dignified accent of education, and he spoke perfect Syrian. "Espresso, without sugar."

"I'll have the same," Shaklam said, and Sandof echoed his order.

The waiter turned to Cyrus. "And you, sir?"

Cyrus grabbed the waiter's arm. "You look like Mahmoud's boy."

The waiter nodded, a flicker of surprise crossing his face. "He taught me everything about coffee before the last bombing."

Cyrus nodded. "Mahmoud was a good man. He always kept the customers away from my table."

The waiter bowed. "And I will do the same."

Their cups were no sooner empty than the waiter took them away and returned with refills. Customers were beginning to exit, leaving the café almost empty.

Once the tables cleared, Cyrus leaned forward, steam rising from his new drink, though it remained untouched.

"As you know, DeathMaster developed a new gaming system. What you don't know is we have an inside man, and he was able to program a way for us to do what we need: to teleport to anyplace we want in the real world."

Cyrus's tone carried a ray of hope.

"More importantly, he built in a way to escape. All we need to do is put the plan in motion."

Rizwan signaled for a third cup of espresso. "If you want us to risk our lives, we need details. I'm not going into this blindly."

"Good enough," Cyrus said. "Remember the old RPG games we played, the ones with certain places in the game where you could teleport to other areas?"

Shaklam pushed his cup away and smiled. "I wasted half my teenage years on those games."

Cyrus leaned forward and lowered his voice. "As I said, what our man programmed in is even better than the old video games. We can teleport to real world locations, using GPS coordinates. In other words, if we know where someone will be, we can teleport there, kill them, and disappear before anyone can find us."

Rizwan's eyes went wide. "What?"

Sandof leaned forward, whispering. "How?"

Cyrus smiled. "For it to work, we must have a system at the destination, and it has to be close - fifty meters at most."

He looked at the others one at a time. "Another limitation is we can only teleport from one spot in the game."

Rizwan perked up. "So we need to get tournament ready?"

Cyrus nodded. "The optimal time to get both targets will coincide with the tournament finals, so we must be good enough to reach the finals, otherwise we'll have no access."

Sandof shook his head. "We should stick to the old ways."

A scowl formed on Cyrus's face. "You'd rather do a suicide mission? Leave more orphans behind?"

Rizwan scoffed at Sandof's suggestion. "They are called 'old ways' for a reason - they're for old men."

"I don't know why we're the ones doing this," Sandof said.

Cyrus clenched his fists, his knuckles whitening. He ground his teeth audibly, and while staring at the wall, the café sounds faded as his eyes lost focus ...

Chapter Two
FLASHBACK - SYRIAN WAR

Cyrus and his twin brother, Tariq, ran down the street, kicking a ball. The street was bathed in afternoon light, and the laughter of many children echoed off stone walls weathered by centuries and not yet scarred by modern weapons.

Young Cyrus, only eight-years old, kicked a worn leather ball to his twin brother. They were identical, except for a small birthmark above Cyrus's lip. Even their movements were synchronized, a dance perfected over years of shared existence, and playing the same game day after day.

Tariq laughed, and shouted to Cyrus. "Kick it higher."

The scent of roasted lamb and garlic wafted from an open window, and the distant call to prayer echoed through the streets.

Cyrus kicked the ball with all his might. "Try to get that, brother."

Tariq ran backward, eyes upward, arms outstretched. As he neared the end of the street, a whistling sound cut through the air, distant at first, then terrifyingly close.

The ground trembled, and dust shook loose from the walls.

Cyrus screamed as the missile hit just meters from Tariq. The deafening sound only hinted at the destruction: concrete shattered, glass imploded - and bodies were blown apart, blood splattering everywhere.

Cyrus was knocked backward, his ears ringing. The world moved in slow motion as he scrambled to his feet.

Where Tariq brother stood was now a smoking crater. Fragments of cloth, flesh, and bone were scattered across the street — unrecognizable except for a small scrap of fabric with a familiar pattern, a birthday gift they had both received.

Cyrus screamed as the ground vibrated again. More missiles hit elsewhere in the city.

Cyrus ran home, his bare feet bleeding on debris-strewn streets, his tears cutting clean tracks through the dust on his face.

Chapter Three
RETURN TO THE CAFÉ

Year 2044

Cyrus's coffee had gone cold, almost as cold as his stare, and no one dared question him.

He glared at Sandof. "We're doing this because we can. Besides, it's been almost fifty years. If this is to end, we need to do it."

Sandof pounded his fist on the table, rattling the cups and saucers. The sound echoed through the nearly empty café. "And to get that pig of a president who supports anyone who is against us."

Sandof looked at each of them, his eyes moving from Rizwan to Shaklam, then back to Cyrus. "In case you don't remember, my cousin was your sister's husband, and the father of her children. Children who are now orphans thanks to that pig."

Sandof lowered his head and nodded to Cyrus. His voice dropped to barely above a whisper. "I understand why you feel the way you do, but we should let Darius and his team handle it."

Cyrus contained his resentment, though his jaw clenched tight enough that the muscles in his face twitched. "You want Darius to do this?"

The words hung in the air like a threat.

The few customers still at the café sensed the change in atmosphere. They hurried to leave, some dropping coins on their tables without waiting for change, others simply abandoning their unfinished drinks. Within moments, the café was empty except for the four of them and the waiter, who disappeared into the back room.

Cyrus reached inside his jacket with deliberate slowness. His fingers found the grip of his gun, and he pulled it free. The metal caught the afternoon light filtering through the bullet-riddled walls. He pointed it at Sandof's head, the movement almost gentle until he began to squeeze. The hammer drew back with a soft, mechanical click.

Sandof's eyes widened. Sweat formed on his forehead and ran down his left cheek, tracing a path through the dust that seemed to coat everything in Damascus these days. His hands drooped to his side, and he trembled. His breath came in short, shallow gasps.

"I guess we'll do this ourselves," Sandof said, his voice barely steady.

Cyrus held the gun steady for three more heartbeats. The only sound was the distant rumble of traffic and the faint buzz of flies near the window. Then slowly, very slowly, he lowered the weapon.

"Yes, we'll do it ourselves."

He tucked the gun back in his waistband, adjusting his shirt to cover it. When he looked up, his expression had softened slightly, though his eyes remained hard.

"But first, we have to deal with the GhostWalkers. They will likely be our opponent." He paused, letting the words sink in. "If we can't beat a team of American teenagers in a game, we have no business going after their president. The tournament gives us cover, gives us access, and gives us the means to escape. But only if we're good enough to reach the finals."

Rizwan leaned forward. "Then we practice until we can't be beaten."

Cyrus nodded. "Exactly."

Chapter Four
CYPRESS HIGH SCHOOL

2044 — Weeks later

Joey Lugullo, 17, talkative and all smiles, strutted down the hall, moving from one class to another. His buddies, Ritchie McGill, 17, with hair cropped short, walked by his side. Ritchie had a sarcastic wit, and he was usually pessimistic. Pete Moritz, 18, trailed them by a few steps. Pete was opinionated and dramatic.

Joey's brother Tony, 15, focused, observant, sometimes blunt, and not developed socially, lagged behind, his head lowered. Headphones hung around his neck, blaring music as he walked.

The hallway buzzed with the chaos of class change. Students rushed past, shouting to friends, slamming lockers, checking phones. The fluorescent lights overhead flickered occasionally, casting uneven shadows across the worn tile floor.

Joey, enthusiastic as always, spoke loudly enough to be heard over the noise. "Don't forget, slackers, we have a game this weekend."

Pete playfully punched Joey's arm, rolling his eyes. "You remind us every damn hour."

"I know these are only practice sessions, but we already lost one, and we can't afford to lose another."

Ritchie adjusted his backpack and sighed. "Count me in, but we can forget winning. Chad's not playing."

Joey stopped dead in his tracks, his expression crumbling. Students bumped into him from behind, muttering complaints as they flowed around him like water around a stone.

"Chad's not playing? Christ's sake. When did he tell you?"

"Last night. His parents are making him focus on his grades," Ritchie said.

"We got no chance without him," Pete added, shaking his head.

Tony stepped forward, weaving between his brother and Pete. His eyes were shining and his voice brimmed with confidence. "I can do it."

Pete crossed his arms and laughed, the sound sharp and dismissive. "Yeah, sure."

Tony's eyes narrowed as he stepped closer to Pete, closing the distance until they were almost chest to chest. "Last season I scored the winning shot when Chad was out. You afraid I'll show you up, Moritz?"

Brief tension erupted. A few students slowed down to watch, sensing a possible confrontation.

Then Ritchie interjected, stepping between them. "If Tony's in, who's out?"

Joey's brow furrowed. He glared at Tony, who held his ground, his jaw set and his shoulders squared.

"I'll challenge any of you, including Joey. If I win, I play."

Joey spoke as if he'd made up his mind, though his voice carried an edge of doubt. "Tony can be backup for now, and since Chad quit, he's out for good. If Tony performs, he's got a spot."

"That's bullshit," Pete said, his face reddening.

Joey glared. "That's the way it is, Pete. Deal with it."

Joey and Ritchie turned down a hallway lined with floor-to-ceiling lockers on both sides. The sound of metal against metal reverberated through the halls as locker doors were slammed closed, and the chatter of teens filled the air. Someone's phone blared music until a teacher yelled for them to turn it off.

Pete and Tony turned left down a long hallway. The crowd thinned out here, with most students heading toward the main exit. About midway down, a group of girls passed by, smiling and giggling among themselves.

A cute girl with auburn hair broke away from her friends and smiled at Tony. "Tony, are you going to the dance?"

The auburn-haired girl's blonde companion stepped closer, her smile seductive. "Hey, Tony."

Tony nodded once, his expression unchanged, and kept walking. He didn't even slow his pace.

The girls exchanged glances, then giggled again as they continued down the hall.

Pete looked at him and shook his head, watching the girls walk away. "Goddamn, that's the third girl that's hit on you today."

When Tony didn't respond, Pete tried again, louder this time. "Christ, talk to them. Do something. They're interested in you."

Tony kept his eyes forward, his headphones still around his neck, music bleeding out loud enough for Pete to hear the bass.

Pete slowed down as Joey raced to catch up to him, his sneakers squeaking on the polished floor.

Out of breath, Joey spoke in halting speech. "I've decided. Tony's playing, so you need to get used to it. Besides, there's no way he won't perform."

Pete looked ahead at Tony, who was now several steps in front of them, oblivious to their conversation. He yelled to him. "That right, Tony?"

When he got no answer, he yelled louder, cupping his hands around his mouth. "Tony, is that right?"

Still nothing. Tony walked on as if he were alone in the hallway.

Pete turned to Joey, exasperation clear on his face. "Christ, is he deaf?"

Joey shrugged, a slight smile playing at his lips. "He's probably got his headphones tuned to some weird damn music. Some noises mess with his head, and he can't focus. When he's like this, he tunes everything else out."

Pete squinted as he looked at Joey questioningly. "What do you mean, 'noises mess with his head'?"

Joey lowered his voice, glancing ahead to make sure Tony was still out of earshot. "Christ, he's autistic. You know that."

Pete's expression shifted from confusion to concern. "Then how the hell is he going to play? I mean, if sounds bother him and he zones out like this..."

Joey stopped and turned to face Pete, his expression serious now. "He's got abilities that make him a lot better than the rest of us, especially as a sniper. Trust me on this."

"And you think Tony's our best chance?"

"Nobody can pull off kill shots like him. I've watched him practice. It's like he sees things we don't, calculates things in his head that would take us forever to figure out."

Ritchie had been tagging along, listening but remaining silent. Now he spoke up. "I just thought he was weird. You know, quiet and stuff."

Pete turned sharply, his eyes flashing. "You shouldn't be talking about weird, Ritchie."

Ritchie's face flushed red. "What's that supposed to mean?"

"It means you live in a glass house, man. We all got our shit."

The bell rang, signaling that they had three minutes to get to their next class. The hallway began to empty as students scattered in different directions.

Joey clapped both of them on the shoulders. "Look, we're a team. Tony's in, and we're going to make this work. Practice is at my place tonight. Seven o'clock. Don't be late."

He jogged off down the hall, leaving Pete and Ritchie standing there.

Ritchie adjusted his backpack again. "You really think Tony can do this?"

Pete watched Tony disappear around a corner, still lost in his own world. "I guess we're about to find out."

Chapter Five
DEATHMASTER

Rick Tilson, 50, with a full head of hair and a stoic expression, stood and greeted Ernie Prelle, 45, cynical and someone who questioned everything.

"Your message said it was important," Rick said.

Ernie closed the door behind him and crossed the spacious office. Floor-to-ceiling windows overlooked downtown Seattle, but neither man paid attention to the view.

"We've had another increase in complaints — tens of thousands more. People are tired of the login issues."

Rick leaned against his desk, arms crossed. "We've still got the best game on the market."

"For now."

Ernie sat in a chair across from Rick, dropping a thick folder onto the desk between them. "And therein lies the problem. We've increased the customer base by almost tenfold, but that increase — while it did great things for our bottom line — exposed us to other problems."

Rick picked up the folder and flipped it open. Charts and graphs showed complaint trends, user satisfaction scores declining, and competitor analysis.

Ernie paused and stared at Rick. "We have major issues with passwords and extensive login problems, and the continual hacking makes everything worse. The customers won't put up with it for long."

"How long do we have?"

"Six months, maybe a year before we start losing serious market share. The forums are already filling up with people threatening to switch to competitors."

Rick tossed the folder back onto the desk. "Hackers are a problem everywhere. Got any ideas?"

Ernie leaned forward, his eyes lighting up with the intensity Rick recognized from their early days building the company. "We've been working on it, and I think we can solve it. If we're successful, we'll have the world by the balls — by the goddamn balls."

"I'm listening."

Ernie handed Rick a printout showing his report. The pages were covered in technical diagrams, security protocols, and implementation timelines.

Rick paced the office, his shoes making soft sounds on the hardwood floor. He nodded as he read the report, occasionally stopping to reread a section or study a diagram more closely.

"Biometric authentication," Rick said, still reading.

"DNA-based login. Completely unique to each user. No passwords to remember, no login credentials to steal, no way for hackers to break in."

Rick looked up from the report. "You're talking about a massive infrastructure overhaul."

"I am. But look at the projections on page seven."

Rick flipped to the page. His eyebrows raised as he scanned the numbers. "These savings are real?"

"Conservative estimates. We eliminate almost all customer service calls related to login issues. We eliminate password reset protocols entirely. We cut our security team needs by sixty percent because we're not constantly fighting credential stuffing attacks and brute force attempts."

"And the customer experience?"

Ernie stood and moved to the window, looking out at the city below. "Instant. They touch the sensor, the system reads their DNA, and they're in. Three seconds, maybe four. Compare that to the current average of two minutes dealing with password managers, two-factor authentication, and inevitable reset requests."

Rick set the report down and walked to stand beside Ernie. "What about privacy concerns? People are already nervous about giving us their DNA."

"We're not storing actual DNA sequences. We're storing a mathematical hash derived from specific genetic markers. It's a one-way encryption. Even if someone stole our database, they couldn't reverse-engineer anyone's DNA from it."

"The press won't understand that distinction."

"Then we educate them. We make it transparent. We show them exactly how it works and why it's safer than anything else on the market."

Rick was quiet for a moment, thinking. "Cost?"

"Eighteen million for development and implementation. Another twelve for the hardware rollout — we'll need to ship sensors to existing customers and build them into new systems."

"Thirty million."

"Against projected savings of eighty million over three years, plus the competitive advantage of being first to market with truly unhackable authentication."

Rick returned to his desk and sat down, studying the report again. "What's the timeline?"

"Nine months for full development and testing. Three months for rollout. We could have the first systems in customer hands within a year."

"Too long. Competitors are moving."

Ernie turned from the window. "If we rush it and it fails, we're done. The backlash would kill us. But if we do this right, we own the market for the next decade."

Rick tapped his fingers on the desk, a habit Ernie recognized as his thinking mode. The office was silent except for the muffled sounds of traffic from the street below.

"You're onto something big," Rick finally said. "Get this to work, and we're golden. Nobody will be able to touch us."

He stood and paced behind his desk, energy building in his movements. "Pull everybody off whatever they're working on and concentrate on this. It takes priority over everything. I don't care about the new maps, the weapon updates, the cosmetic items. This is survival."

"What about the Christmas release?"

"Push it. Tell marketing to spin it as quality control. Tell them we're perfecting the experience."

Ernie smiled and stood to leave. All that was missing was a salute. He picked up his folder and headed for the door.

"Ernie."

He stopped and turned back.

Rick looked at him seriously. "Don't screw this up. This company's future is riding on it."

"I know."

"And one more thing. Keep it quiet. If word gets out before we're ready, every competitor will race to copy it. I want to announce this when we're ready to ship, not a day before."

"Understood."

Ernie left the office, closing the door softly behind him. Rick stood at his window, looking out at the city, already thinking about the press conference, the marketing campaign, the future of the company.

Thirty million was a lot to bet on one project.

But Ernie had never let him down before.

Chapter Six
LUGULLO HOUSE

The doorbell rang and Joey rushed to answer it. Pete and Ritchie stood on the porch, smoking cigarettes.

Joey shook his head. "Get the hell in here, assholes; It's raining."

Ritchie smirked. "Says the man who took so long to answer the door."

Joey held the door open while Pete and Ritchie wiped their feet on the mat.

Pete seemed eager to start playing. "Let's get going. I don't have all night. My old man will be stalking me soon."

Joey led them down the hall. "You better practice first 'cause I'm gonna kick your ass."

Pete chortled. "What we need is competition. We already beat the best teams out there."

Pete plopped on the sofa alongside Ritchie and Joey. He picked up a remote control and pretended to press buttons rapidly with his thumbs.

Tony grabbed a remote and a headset and sat on the floor. Pete, Ritchie, and Joey donned their gear, then lit cigarettes and started playing. The cigarettes dangled from the left side of their mouths as they played.

Tony brushed his hand in the air and coughed. Then he got up and opened the window.

"Put those things out. Christ, Joey, my asthma is killing me. I can barely breathe."

"I'll put my smoke out if you close that damn window. It's raining like hell out there," Ritchie said.

All of them sat up straight and gripped their controllers. They mashed the buttons which were used to move and fire weapons, among other functions.

Pete grabbed his remote and took a spot on the floor.

"You hear the news? DeathMaster announced that a revolutionary new system is on the way. Even better, whichever team wins the new tournament will get a system for each team member, including backup players."

"I thought they'd be giving money. I'd rather have that," Ritchie said.

"No, idiot. You get the money and the system."

"Then we better get practicing."

"Get practicing is right because no matter who we face in the tournament, they'll be good. Damn good. And I intend to win a major tournament before wasting my life in college," Joey said.

"Who you think we'll be up against?"

"I'm guessing WolfDen, but we won't know until the semifinals are over."

After they enter Joey's room, Pete plopped on the sofa alongside Ritchie and Joey. He picked up a remote control and pretended to press buttons rapidly with his thumbs.

Tony, already sitting in his favorite beanbag, grabbed a remote and a headset.

Pete, Ritchie, and Joey donned their gear, then lit cigarettes. The cigarettes dangled from their mouths as they played.

Tony brushed his hand in the air and coughed. "Put those things out. I can barely breathe."

Joey smacked the sofa with the palm of his hand. "Sit tight. I've got goddamn login problems — again."

"They need to fix this shit," Ritchie said.

A loud knock was heard at the door, and Joey's mother, Missy Lugullo, 40, always calm, logical and concerned, hollered into the room. "If I hear any more of that language, I'll switch the circuit breaker off."

Joey yelled back. "You got it, Mom."

Joey looked at the others and grinned, then whispered to Pete and Ritchie. "Y'all need to watch your mouth, 'cause she'll do it."

Pete raised a hand to his mouth and gestured that he'd zip his lips closed, causing the others to laugh.

"Get ready," Joey said. "It looks like I'm logged in."

All of them sat up straight and gripped their controls. They mashed the buttons which were used to move and fire weapons, among other functions.

"Y'all need to get your shit together," Joey said. "We've got a tournament coming up."

Pete kept firing, but responded sarcastically. "That's more than six months away, so stop worrying. We'll be ready."

After nearly four hours of playing, the door opened and Missy poked her head in. "Don't you think it's about time to wrap things up? It *is* a school night."

Joey continued mashing the buttons on his controller. "Ten more minutes, Mom. I swear."

"All right. But ten minutes is all you're getting."

They successfully defeated the competition, high-fived each other, then Pete and Ritchie went home.

Chapter Seven
THE F.B.I.

Sean Lugullo, 40 and meticulously dressed, parked in the garage of a six-story building and presented his ID to the guard who granted him access. He then removed all metallic objects and passed through the scanner.

The metal detector beeped twice before giving him the all-clear. He'd forgotten to take the keys out of his pocket again. The guard, a heavyset man named Martinez who'd worked the building for fifteen years, waved him through with a knowing smile.

Once through, Sean crossed the tiled floor of the lobby, rode the elevator to the fourth floor, exited, and headed down a long corridor to his office. The fluorescent lights overhead hummed with their constant electrical buzz, and the faint smell of industrial cleaner lingered in the air.

He unlocked the door and sat at his desk, which was immaculate. Even his trash can was clean. Everything had its place: pens lined up parallel to the desk edge, files stacked by priority, coffee mug positioned precisely on a coaster.

The phone rang incessantly, but he ignored it and focused on the computer monitor. He was reviewing case files from the overnight shift, looking for patterns, connections, anything that might have been missed.

Joan, a competent assistant in her 30s who was always polite but stern, poked her head in the door and knocked to get Sean's attention.

"Mr. Lugullo, your phone is ringing."

Without looking up, he waved her off. "I heard it."

Joan stood in the doorway, hands on her hips. She wasn't going anywhere until he picked up.

"All right. All right," Sean said, reaching for the receiver. "I'll get it."

Joan nodded and pulled the door closed behind her.

Sean picked up the phone. "Lugullo."

Director Samuels' voice carried urgency. "We've got a potential situation, so we'll need you to be on hand — day and night."

Sean sat up straighter, his full attention now on the call. He grabbed a pen and pulled a notepad closer. "What kind of situation?"

"The CIA picked up chatter from an unknown cell, and it came across as real. From what we've deciphered, they are hinting at a high-level assassination."

"Shit, that doesn't sound good. Any idea who?"

"So far, they don't know who they plan on targeting. Even worse, they don't know who's planning it. It could be a Syrian operation or an Iranian one. Either one is a viable option, so keep your team alert."

Sean wrote "Syria/Iran" on his notepad and underlined it twice. "What makes you think it's them?"

"We've been at odds with them for almost fifty years. Remember when we killed their leaders and overthrew the regimes?"

"Unfortunately, I do, but I thought that was over."

Director Samuels gave a bitter laugh. "Those emotions are tough to bury, and when you do, there's a danger they'll erupt at any time. We've been monitoring increased chatter from both regions over the past six months. References to revenge, and settling old scores. Most of it's just noise, but this feels different."

"Different how?"

"It's organized. They're being careful with their communications, using encryption we haven't seen before. That level of operational security suggests this isn't just talk."

Sean made more notes. "Any specifics on who they're targeting? Or their location?"

"Not yet. They're using encrypted phones, and they're in hostile territory, so it's tough to track. NSA is working on breaking their codes, but it's slow going. What we do know is they've mentioned timelines. Something about 'when the time is right' and 'after the tournament.'"

"What tournament?"

"No idea. It could be code for something else, or it could be literal. We're running it through every database we have."

Sean circled the word "tournament" on his notepad. "What about potential targets? If this is revenge for regime change, we're talking about high-value political figures."

"That's our assumption. We've already increased security around the President, the Secretary of State, the Vice President, and several former intelligence directors who were involved in those operations. But without more specific intel, we're shooting in the dark."

"How many people are we looking at in this cell?"

"Unknown. The intercepts suggest at least four, maybe more. They're disciplined, professional. This isn't amateur hour."

Sean felt the familiar tightening in his chest that came with major threat assessments. "What resources do I get?"

"You'll have whatever you need. I'm authorizing overtime for your entire team. I want eyes on every piece of intelligence that comes through. I want daily briefings. And I want to know the second we get anything actionable."

"Understood. I'll brief my team this afternoon."

"One more thing, Lugullo. Keep this compartmentalized. Need-to-know only. If this leaks and we spook them, they'll go dark."

"You have my cell and home numbers, sir. I'm reachable at all times."

"Good. Because if this is what I think it is, we're on a clock."

After the line went dead, Sean sat back in his chair and stared at his notes. Syria. Iran. Assassination. Tournament. Four words that didn't make sense together, but somehow they were connected.

He picked up his phone and dialed his team lead. "Carter, it's Lugullo. I need everyone in the conference room in thirty minutes no matter what they're doing. This takes priority."

He hung up and looked at the photo on his desk. Missy and the boys, taken last summer at the beach. Joey was making a face at the camera. Tony was looking off to the side, probably distracted by something in the sand.

Fifty years of bad blood, he thought. And now someone is ready to collect.

He closed the case file on his computer and opened a new folder. This one he labeled: UNKNOWN THREAT - PRIORITY ONE.

Then he got up and headed to the conference room. It was going to be a long day.

And probably a longer month.

Chapter Eight
A NEW SYSTEM

DeathMaster headquarters — San Jose — three months later

Ernie entered Rick's office, plopped down in the leather chair across from the desk, and sighed. His shirt was wrinkled, his tie loosened, and dark circles shadowed his eyes.

Rick glanced at him and smiled. "Late night?"

"Always, but I think it's paying off. It looks like we've had a breakthrough, and it's just in time. We've got a big tournament coming up."

Rick rested his elbows on the desk and leaned forward. The afternoon sun streamed through the floor-to-ceiling windows behind him. "Let's hear it."

"The engineering team thinks — and I emphasize thinks — they have a foolproof way to solve both problems: login issues and hacking."

Rick raised an eyebrow. Over the past three months, he'd heard a dozen different proposals from the engineering team. Half of them had been impractical. The other half had been too expensive. He'd learned to temper his expectations.

"I hope you're not talking about fingerprints because that's been tried before, and it's got issues."

Ernie shook his head and smiled. "Not fingerprints — DNA."

"DNA?"

Ernie smiled like the cat that caught the canary. He pulled a folder from his briefcase and slid it across the desk. "They've found a way to grant access based on a person's DNA. They're working on various ways to collect a sample: blood, swabs, sweat, but it looks like it's going to work. Best of all, it's foolproof: no passwords or username problems, and no need to verify who you are. The DNA does it all."

Rick opened the folder and scanned the technical specifications. Pages of diagrams, test results, and implementation plans. His eyes widened as he read the success rates from the initial trials.

"These numbers are real?"

"Ninety-eight percent accuracy in controlled tests. We're aiming for ninety-nine point five before we roll it out."

Rick flipped through more pages. "What about the privacy concerns? People are going to lose their minds when they hear we're collecting DNA."

"We're not collecting DNA sequences. We're creating a mathematical hash from specific genetic markers. It's one-way encryption. Even if someone hacked our servers and stole the database, they couldn't reverse-engineer anyone's actual DNA from it."

"You're sure about that?"

"Positive. I had our security team run every attack scenario they could think of. The hash is unbreakable."

Rick set the folder down and leaned back in his chair. He steepled his fingers and stared at the ceiling, thinking. The office was quiet except for the hum of the air conditioning and the distant sounds of traffic from the street below.

"Cost?" he finally asked.

"We're under budget. The initial development cost us twelve million, but we can implement it for another eight. Total of twenty million, well below our thirty million authorization."

"Timeline?"

"We can have the first systems ready in six weeks. Full rollout in three months if we push hard."

Rick sat forward. "Six weeks puts us right at the tournament."

"Exactly. We could debut it there. Announce it to the world with the biggest prize pool in gaming history. The press coverage alone would be worth millions."

Rick tapped his fingers on the desk, a habit he had when making big decisions. "What if it fails? What if we announce it and something goes wrong?"

"Then we have a backup plan. We run the tournament on the old system and quietly shelve the DNA tech until we can fix whatever broke. But I don't think it will fail. The tests have been rock solid."

"Who knows about this?"

"Just the engineering team. About fifteen people total. I've kept it compartmentalized like you asked."

"Good. Keep it that way."

Rick stood and walked to the window. Below, the parking lot was filling up as the day shift arrived. Cars streamed in, people hurried toward the building, everyone focused on their own tasks, oblivious to the breakthrough happening in the executive suite.

"This could change everything," Rick said, still looking out the window.

"It *will* change everything. No other gaming company has anything close to this. We'll own the market for years."

Rick turned back to face Ernie. "What about international regulations? Different countries have different privacy laws."

"Legal is already on it. We're clear in the U.S., Canada, and most of Europe. Asia's trickier, but we have workarounds. Worst case, we limit the DNA system to certain regions and use traditional authentication elsewhere."

"And the hardware? We need sensors in every system."

"Already designed. Small and non-invasive. It will cost us about eight dollars per unit to manufacture. We can build them into new systems and ship retrofit kits to existing customers."

Rick walked back to his desk and sat down. He picked up the folder again and studied the implementation timeline. "You said six weeks?"

"Six weeks for the tournament systems. Then we start scaling up production."

Rick sat back in his chair and smiled for the first time since Ernie had entered. "You just made my wife happy because I'm going home a relaxed man."

Ernie stood and headed toward the door. He was almost out when Rick called after him.

"Tell the team they'll get a big bonus if they make it happen before the tournament."

Ernie turned back, grinning. "How big?"

"Big enough to make them forget they haven't slept in three months."

"They'll love that."

"And, Ernie — once they get it working, only give a few select groups access to this until we work out any bugs. I want beta testers we can trust. People who'll report problems instead of running to social media."

"Already planned for it. I'm thinking we start with our top-tier tournament players. They're invested in the platform, they understand the tech, and they'll give us honest feedback."

"Perfect. And keep monitoring the privacy angle. The second we get pushback from regulators or advocacy groups, I want to know."

"Will do."

Ernie left, closing the door behind him.

Rick sat alone in his office, the folder still open on his desk. He read through the technical specifications one more time, making sure he hadn't missed anything.

DNA-based authentication. It sounds like science fiction, but the data is solid. The tests are solid and the team is solid.

He looked at the tournament schedule pinned to his wall. Six weeks. The biggest event in competitive gaming history, and they were going to revolutionize the industry right in the middle of it.

He picked up his phone and called his wife. "Hey, honey. I'm coming home early tonight."

"Early? Are you sick?"

He laughed. "Not at all. I just had some good news. Really good news."

"Well, don't keep me in suspense."

"I'll tell you over dinner. Make a reservation somewhere nice. We're celebrating."

He hung up and looked out the window again. The sun was starting to set, painting the sky in shades of orange and pink.

Six weeks and everything changes.

Chapter Nine
THE BIG ANNOUNCEMENT

Kafeh Supreme — Damascus

Cyrus welcomed Rizwan and Sandof into his house, inviting them to sit.

"Shaklam couldn't make it," Rizwan said. "But I'll see him tonight."

Cyrus scowled. "Remind Shaklam that if he misses another meeting, he'll be relieved."

Rizwan nodded. "Now tell us why we're here, Cyrus."

Cyrus plopped on the sofa and turned on the TV. "DeathMaster is about to make an announcement."

Joey sat in his beanbag chair, surrounded by Tony, Pete, and Ritchie.

"Everybody shut the fuck up. The announcement is about to start."

The three of them shifted in their seats, eyes glued to the screen. Pete cracked open an energy drink. Tony adjusted his headphones, lowering them around his neck. Ritchie leaned forward, elbows on his knees.

Cyrus glared as Shaklam entered, his head hung low.

"Don't say anything," Cyrus said, his voice sharp.

Shaklam nodded and took a seat on the floor, keeping his eyes down. Rizwan and Sandof exchanged glances but said nothing.

The screen came into focus and Joey and his team leaned forward, watching intently.

"All right, guys. Here it comes," Joey said.

A crackling sound was heard and then the TV screen showed Rick Tilson standing before DeathMaster's headquarters. He wore a sharp suit and stood at a podium with the company logo behind him. A crowd had gathered, their excited chatter audible in the background.

"Everyone's been waiting a long time for this, so I'm going to get right to it. We have finally got a fix for the incessant login problems and the annoying password issues."

Loud applause was heard in the background.

Rick waited for it to die down before continuing. "Not only that, but our team of brilliant engineers has developed a new system that puts all other systems to shame. In fact, we're so confident you'll enjoy it, that we're offering a guarantee: try it for thirty days, and if you don't like it, you get a full refund."

The applause grew louder. People in the crowd whistled and cheered.

Rick held up his hand, calling for quiet. "I don't know much about the technical details, and Ernie is stuck with the engineers, but he will get with the following teams within a few days. These are the lucky ones who will win a new system for each member, and they'll get to beta-test the new game."

Rick held up a piece of paper and read from it. "WolfDen, Ghost-Walkers, Corner Boys, and last but not least, River Rats."

Cyrus whistled loudly and popped the top on a beer. Foam spilled over the edge and he wiped it with his hand. "I'm guessing we'll be paired with the GhostWalkers, but knowing DeathMaster, the final matchup will be determined by points, not wins."

Rizwan grabbed a can from the fridge. "We need to stop Ghost-Walkers from getting a lot of points. I'd rather not face them twice."

"They don't stand a chance," Sandof said, leaning back in his chair.

Cyrus shot him a look. "Don't underestimate them. They're kids, but they're good. Talented kids with nothing to lose are very dangerous."

Shaklam finally spoke. "What about the new systems? Do we trust them?"

"We don't have a choice," Cyrus said. "If we want access to the tournament, we use their systems. But we'll test them thoroughly before we rely on them for anything important."

Joey high-fived the others in the room, then sat and gloated. His smile stretched from ear to ear.

"It almost don't matter if we win, we still get the system," Ritchie said.

Pete stared as if he were nuts. "Your ass. I'm not about to lose. We're going all the way."

"We'll find out the rest when we get the email, so let's get practicing," Tony said, already pulling on his headset.

Joey grabbed his controller. "Tony's right. We got work to do."

"We'll have to catch up on work later. I need to get home," Pete said.

"Me too," Ritchie said as he stood to leave.

Hours later, Joey checked his messages, then he looked at his email. A message from DeathMaster waited for him. The subject line read: "SEMIFINAL INVITATION - GHOSTWALKERS."

"Tony. DeathMaster sent us an email. It's gotta be about the semifinals."

Tony loomed over Joey's shoulder, squinting at the screen.

"No shit. They just announced we're in. All the email's going to do is confirm it."

Joey clicked the email and it opened, displaying the text on the screen:

"Joseph Lugullo and GhostWalker members: You are invited to participate in the semifinals against Team WolfDen for a chance at the ultimate finals and the grand prize. All final entrants will receive new systems as well as our newly created sensor suits. More instructions to follow."

Joey read it twice, then pumped his fist in the air. "Hot shit. We're gold now. Call Pete. I'll call Ritchie."

Tony pulled out his phone and dialed. "Pete, it's official. We're facing WolfDen in the semis."

Joey was already talking to Ritchie. "Get your ass over here. We need to practice."

"All right, but I need to sneak out."

Pete answered on the first ring. "What's up, Tony?"

"Joey's calling an emergency practice. We got the email from DeathMaster."

"Shit, all right. I'll have to ask if I can stay at your house, so clear it with your parents."

"No problem," Tony said.

Within the hour, the team had reassembled in Joey's bedroom. Controllers out, headsets on, energy drinks lined up within reach.

"We've got two weeks before the semis," Joey said. "That's two weeks to get better than we've ever been."

"WolfDen's good," Tony said. "They've won their last five tournaments."

"Then we'll be better," Joey said.

Back in Damascus, Cyrus stood and addressed his team. "We need to get in as much practice as we can before we face the GhostWalkers. It's no time to be overconfident."

Rizwan nodded. "When do we start?"

"Now. And we don't stop until we're ready."

Shaklam grabbed his controller. "What about the new systems?"

"They'll arrive in a few days. Until then, we practice with what we have. But once they arrive, we switch immediately. We need to know those systems inside and out before the tournament."

Cyrus looked at each of them. "This is what we've been waiting for. Everything we've planned depends on reaching the finals. We can't afford to lose to a team of American teenagers."

"We won't," Sandof said.

"Then prove it. Get your gear and let's get started."

The WolfDen team settled into their positions. The room fell quiet except for the sounds of controllers clicking and the occasional command called out over the comms.

Outside, the sun was setting over Damascus. The city was bathed in orange light, shadows lengthening across the scarred buildings and bullet-riddled walls.

But inside Cyrus's house, four men sat focused on screens, their minds already in another world, preparing for a battle that meant more than anyone else could possibly know.

Chapter Ten
URBAN SPRAWL

The team gathered around the TV that night. Joey and Pete sat on the sofa, and Ritchie and Tony sat on beanbags. Headsets, controllers, and energy drinks were spread within grabbing distance.

Posters of girls in sexy poses, and others of Rambo and John Wick decorated the walls. Ashtrays filled with crushed-out cigarettes sat to the side.

"This is it. Game two starts tonight and we can't afford mistakes. This game takes place in several scenarios, so be ready," Joey said.

Pete rolled his eyes. "Like you'd let us forget."

They entered the Urban Sprawl scenario. The landscape was filled with factories, warehouses, and toxic waste areas. Subway tunnels, elevated trains, multi-level highway systems, and rooftop pathways dotted the terrain.

Joey navigated filthy alleyways while Tony scanned from a rooftop.

"Two enemies approaching from your left," Tony said over the comm.

Joey pressed his back against a graffiti-covered wall. He held his breath as two enemy soldiers passed just feet away.

Joey pulled the trigger twice. The muted sound of the suppressed rifle dropped both of them.

"Good spotting," Joey said.

Tony's avatar offered a virtual thumbs-up from the rooftop as he relocated to a new vantage point.

In the second round at Piney Woods, Pete took cover behind a fallen tree. A branch snapped under his boot. Enemy fire immediately followed, crippling him.

Ritchie heard the fire, popped up from behind a boulder and took both of the enemy soldiers out with kill shots.

"Goddamnit," Pete said over the comm.

"Chill, man. Pretend it's just practice," Joey said.

Pete exploded. "It's never just practice."

In the final round, Joey reported seeing nothing, as did Pete and Ritchie.

Tony lay motionless in a sniper position, scanning with his scope. He stopped at a slight movement in the grass, then an inconsistent shadow, and finally, a faint glint of metal.

Tony calculated their movement and fired - "pfft!" into the grass. Then he shifted the gun slightly - "pfft!" where the shadow should be. Then to a different area entirely - "pfft!"

Three death notifications appeared on screen. The team watched in disbelief as the kill-cam replay showed enemies who were perfectly camouflaged.

"How the hell did you know they were there?" Joey asked

"Patterns. They always follow patterns," Tony said.

The team removed their headsets and sighed.

"I'm exhausted," Ritchie said.

"Don't get excited yet, but we're now even with WolfDen," Joey said.

"Holy shit. We might actually get those new systems," Ritchie said.

"And the prize money and a movie deal," Joey added.

"Only if we win," Tony said.

Pete looked at Tony. "You're the edge we need. Nobody can snipe like you."

Tony was surprised by the compliment. "Thanks ... I think."

"Doesn't matter who gets the credit. We're a team," Joey said.

Sean Lugullo walked into the bedroom carrying a box, and Joey jumped up to get it. He ripped it open and yanked out several plastic-wrapped packages.

"The suits. We got the suits," Joey said.

Chapter Eleven
ANOTHER PRACTICE

Pete and Ritchie stood on the front porch of Joey's house, finishing their smokes. Ritchie crushed his out on the concrete, then Pete took a final drag and tossed his butt onto the front yard.

Joey opened the door before they had a chance to knock.

He led them to his bedroom and opened the door. Three beanbag chairs sat on the floor in front of a 65" big-screen TV and a game station. A stained sofa with torn cushions sat behind them against the wall.

Joey sat on the sofa, and Pete and Ritchie took seats on the beanbags. All of them puffed on their vapes.

Tony entered a moment later, and made a sour face.

"Damn, those vapes stink almost as bad as the real things. Open the window."

Pete turned to look at Joey. "Startin' already."

"It's got nothing to do with his game. Besides, he's got bad asthma, so ditch the vapes. And no more shit, Pete. I made the call; besides, we need a good sniper."

Pete put his vape aside, then nudged Tony with his foot. "Gonna teach us how to lose?"

Tony smiled, leaned back in the beanbag, and crossed his feet. "I'm sure you know all about losing."

Ritchie put his vape away, and turned to the others. "You hear the rumors? DeathMaster is supposed to be coming out with a new system that fixes the login issues."

"If you look at their latest work, I'd bet it'll be DNA based."

Ritchie hit the wall with the palm of his hand. "Hot damn. At least we'll be able to log in without problems."

"But you've got to use your DNA, for Christ's sake," Pete said.

"It's no different than getting a blood test," Tony said. "Not even as bad."

A knock sounded at the door, and in walked Joey's father, Sean Lugullo. He was in his mid-forties with a full head of hair and a serious demeanor.

"I'm giving you a one-hour notice, then lights are out."

"Come on, Dad. I just got to play," Tony said.

"You heard what I said — one hour."

"Come on, Dad. Make it two?"

Sean sighed. "All right, you get two but no more."

Tony smacked the floor and pursed his lips.

"Thanks, Dad," Joey said.

Joey turned to the others. "Let's make use of the time. This is our last chance to practice, and we're only getting this because the suits aren't ready yet."

"When are they coming?" Ritchie asked.

"Supposed to be here by tomorrow — DNA-linked, full-body, haptic sensor suits."

"I know Joey didn't read the material, so I'll tell you," Tony said. "Thousands of sensors are embedded in the suit, and they'll detect impact and pressure changes. The effect is the suit will simulate being shot, stabbed, heat from an injury, and more. It won't be as bad as the real thing, but it will hurt like hell."

"And you didn't tell us the biggest news, Joey," Pete said.

"What?"

"The prizes: $25,000 to the winning team, new systems for every player, and a goddamn movie deal."

"Holy shit. I can go to college with that much money," Ritchie said.

Pete laughed. "I think college costs a lot more."

Chapter Twelve
DESERT SANDS SCENARIO

Syria

The new systems arrived, along with the suits to be worn when playing. Cyrus called the team members to his house, and they prepared to practice.

"We'll be up against the Corner Boys, and we'll be rated on how well we perform. The GhostWalkers will be against the River Rats. If it goes as I suspect, our next game will be against the GhostWalkers."

Cyrus stared at each of them. "But don't underestimate the Corner Boys. They didn't get this far by being slackers."

The WolfDen team entered the Desert Sands scenario and immediately spread out. There was a small fortress surrounded by an endless expanse of sand, and one small oasis.

They took up positions behind tall dunes, and behind palm trees in the oasis, their suits camouflaged to blend into the surroundings. The team split, and the units slowly advanced toward the enemy targets on the east and west side of the fortress.

The Corner Boys moved awkwardly; they seemed out of their element in the Desert Sands scenario.

Rizwan and Cyrus advanced on the western side of the fortress, their targets in sight, Rizwan stayed low, only lifting his head to spot them as they approached. Once they were close enough, he sighted them in and fired three times in rapid succession. Two of them went down, leaving two remaining.

Rizwan spoke into his mic. "Western side cleared."

"We're good to go," Sandoz said. He and Shaklam advanced from the east and entered the fortress. Once inside, they opened the gates, allowing Rizwan and Cyrus to enter. Cyrus then stalked the remaining targets and annihilated them.

Chapter Thirteen
PINEY WOODS SCENARIO

Houston

Team GhostWalkers donned their headsets and grabbed the controllers in Joey's bedroom. "We'll be playing the River Rats today, but don't get cocky; they're good enough to beat us on any day."

"They're all hype," Ritchie said.

Joey shook his head. "Okay, it's time to kick ass. Set your frequency to 165. Repeat, 165."

Joey tapped Pete and Ritchie on the shoulder. "Remember, with this new system, you'll feel it if you get shot or stabbed. It won't be the same as the real thing, but it'll hurt."

Joey sneaked through the eastern forest in the Piney Woods scenario, using trees for cover. He stopped every few feet to listen for sounds of the enemy.

Pete advanced from the western flank, mimicking Joey's movements. He carried an automatic, shooting .223 rounds.

Ritchie slowly moved up from the rear, covering the south side, and Tony lay flat on a sniper stand, high in the trees. He used an Accuracy International Sniper Rifle, and he seldom missed.

Tony moved his scope slowly, surveilling the area from east to west. He then checked north to south.

"Got three incoming, heading straight for Joey."

"Ritchie, can you provide cover? I can get one or two, but I doubt I can get all three."

"I'll take the one in the lead," Ritchie said. "I'm advancing now."

Tony zeroed in on the one furthest west. "Fire on my signal."

Tony waited for him to get a bit closer. "Now." He shot, taking the target out with a shot to the chest.

Ritchie hit his mark in the leg, then panicked and rushed his advance. When he stood, he was shot in the thigh.

"Goddamn. Son of a bitch. I'm hit."

Pete moved from behind a tree and took out the enemy who hit Ritchie, then he ducked. "Take cover. There's still one left."

"I spot him approaching from the south," Tony said. "I'm gonna let him get closer before I shoot, so stay hidden."

The enemy crawled on his belly through the woods. When he reached the edge, near a clearing, he paused. Tony focused his scope, and when the target moved forward, he took his shot.

"Headshot. That clears them out."

The GhostWalkers removed their headsets and turned the system off. "How's that for someone who can't play?"

"You just got lucky," Pete said, and lit a cigarette. "If that were a real game Ritchie would have cost us a point. And Christ, did you hear him wail when he got hit? You would have thought it was a real bullet."

Joey high-fived all of the team. "All right, guys. Enough trash-talking. We scored a win tonight, which was good, but we need to keep practicing if we hope to beat WolfDen, and we've only got a few weeks."

Pete nodded. "We'll be ready, don't worry, but right now I've got to get my ass home." He got up, opened the door, and left. "See you tomorrow."

"Yeah, I gotta go too," Ritchie said. "See y'all at school."

Pete strutted down the hall at Cypress Middle School, rap music blaring from his headsets. Several friends passed by and fist-bumped him.

Shorty, seventeen and beanpole thin with a Chicago accent, rounded the corner. He shot Pete a shit-eating grin. "Hey, Pete, what's up? Worried about the next game?"

"Not if you're the competition."

Shorty brushed him off. "Keep thinkin' that, Moritz."

Joey turned into the hallway where Pete was. "Pete, don't forget we're practicing tonight."

"I know. And we better get good. I just saw Shorty, and he seemed real confident."

"He's got a right to be. I watched them practice, and they got this new member named Brie, and she's pretty damn good."

"Pretty damn good or pretty damn hot?"

"Maybe both."

Pete walked closer to Joey. "You think she could replace Ritchie?"

"I'm not ready to ditch Ritchie yet, but we'll keep her in mind. Let's watch them compete, see if they've got anything to feel pumped about."

Joey, Pete, Tony, and Ritchie sat on beanbags in Joey's bedroom and stared at the screen.

"There's Shorty," Pete said. "He's in the lead position."

"And here comes Brie," Joey said. "She's getting in position as the sniper."

Tony stood and opened the door. "I'm grabbing a snack. Call me if anything good happens."

"Sit down. You need to watch this team and see what you think. We might have to play them."

"C'mon, Joey. All you're watching is Brie's ass."

"All right, everyone lay off Brie's ass and focus on the game. We need practice. Let's get together tomorrow after school."

Joey unpacked the new boxes and read the instructions on the system and suits. He took a long drag on his cigarette while Tony sat in the beanbag chair.

Pete and Ritchie walked in, laughing.

"What's up, dudes?"

"I'll tell you what's up — we got our new systems and suits today."

"What? When? What's new?" Ritchie asked.

"Where are they?"

"Here's the bottom line: The sensor suit is brand new with a lot of new technology. Don't ask me how, but it uses our DNA to allow us access to the game, and that somehow lets them make the game almost real."

Joey paused.

"If you get injured while playing, you will feel the wound. It won't be as intense as in the real world, but it'll still hurt. All shots are monitored and registered, so depending on where you're hit, you may be dismissed."

Joey pointed at Ritchie. "And everybody's got to wear protective gear to cover the head, neck, and other sensitive parts."

Another pause.

"One more thing: remember the save spots in the old games? In this game, they're used to teleport you from one spot to another. That's a key strategy, so we need to get used to it."

"What's it say about the prizes? What do we win?"

"First, we have to win."

Joey scanned the second paper he held. "Second place gets five thousand dollars for each team, and first place gets twenty-five thousand."

Pete perked up. "Twenty-five grand. No shit."

"We're gonna be goddamn rich," Ritchie said.

"Wait, there's more. The first-place team also gets a movie made by a major studio."

"Holy shit. That does it," Ritchie said. "We're practicing every night."

"How the hell does the DNA work?"

"No idea, but I guess we'll find out."

"Who the hell cares?" Ritchie asked. "It's twenty-five grand."

Chapter Fourteen
HOW TO TELEPORT

Damascus

Cyrus glared at Shaklam as he entered the house without removing his shoes.

Shaklam held his head low as he stepped out of his sandals. He was about to speak when Cyrus held his hand up, palm facing Shaklam.

"We got the suits today. That means the rest of the tournament will seem more real, and it *will* be more real. When you get shot, it will hurt — a lot."

Sandof smiled. "And the GhostWalkers aren't used to pain."

Cyrus popped open a beer. "I told you before not to underestimate them, but regardless, we have a slight advantage over the GhostWalkers. They're kids, but they're smart kids, so the advantage is only slight."

"They'll be no problem," Sandof said.

"Don't be a fool, Sandof. On any given day, they're as good as we are. Act like it."

He paused. "And remember, the only way to use the teleport station is to not let *them* control it."

"I thought we needed access to a particular scenario to teleport," Sandof said.

"Our associate will make sure that scenario is played when we need it."

He looked around at the team. "That doesn't mean we have easy access to the station. We still have to defend the position."

Two nights later, Pete and Ritchie walked into Joey's bedroom, laughing. Pete patted the butt of a near-naked girl portrayed on a poster hanging on the wall.

"What's up, dudes?"

Joey tossed a suit to Pete and Ritchie. "You're late, that's what's up."

Tony spoke nonchalantly from his beanbag on the floor. "Don't forget, with these suits, if you get shot in the game, you feel it for real."

Joey pointed to a diagram in the booklet. "And check this, a teleportation station just like they said. It's like the old RPGs we played, but there's only one, and it's in the Piney Woods scenario."

Tony examined his suit, covered in advanced sensors. It even covered the feet. He put his headsets on and read the instructions. "We'll feel everything with these suits, even what we step on. This changes everything."

He paused.

"Using our DNA, the suits will transfer any hits into pain. It says here a shot will feel like a strong paintball hit. It'll hurt, but it won't be bad."

"It'll still hurt like hell," Joey said. "Now get ready. The game starts in an hour. Let's see what these babies can do."

"We need to practice every night," Ritchie said. "I'm goin' to college."

Pete shook his head and laughed. "Keep dreaming."

Piney Woods Scenario

Dense clusters of tall pines were packed close together making it difficult to navigate, and the morning fog hanging between the trees made it difficult to see. The ground was covered with pine needles, and broken branches ensured sound traveled unpredictably — sometimes muffled, sometimes not.

Joey sneaked through the eastern forest, using trees for cover. He stopped every few feet to listen for sounds of the enemy.

Pete advanced from the western flank, mimicking Joey's movements. He carried an automatic, shooting .223 rounds.

Pete took aim at a target, but slipped, snapping branches, which drew the enemy's attention. They took him out with one shot.

Ritchie slowly moved from the rear, covering the south side. He carried the newest assault rifle.

Tony lay flat on a sniper stand, high in the trees. He used an Accuracy International AS50 and he seldom missed.

As night fell over the Piney Woods, the fighting continued.

A message scrolled across the screen in big letters: **FIFTEEN MINUTE BREAK**.

Pete slammed his controller onto the floor and punched the beanbag.

"Goddamnit."

"Chill, man," Joey said.

Pete fumed. "That's the second time I screwed up. It's not acceptable."

"Your dad messing with you again?"

Pete closed his eyes and pursed his lips, then he nodded and breathed deeply. "You know how he is. After three tours in Afghanistan, he thinks games are for kids."

Pete laughed bitterly. "I can't wait to see the look on his face when we win."

Tony got up and headed for the door.

"Where you going?" Joey asked.

"Takin' a piss. That's why they have breaks, Joey. Damn."

. . .

Tony returned and fluffed up his beanbag, then took a seat.

A message flashed on the screen and a beeping noise was heard.

"Break's over. Let's get back to it," Tony said.

He slowly scoped the area, surveilling it from east to west. He then checked north to south.

"Got three incoming, heading straight for Joey."

Tony paused. "Ritchie, can you provide cover? I can get two, but not three."

"I'll take the one in the lead. Advancing now."

"Fire on my signal."

Tony zeroed in on the one furthest west.

"Now."

He fired, taking the target out with a shot to the chest. Ritchie hit his mark in the leg, then panicked and rushed his advance. When he stood, he was shot in the thigh.

"Goddamn, I'm hit. Son of a bitch."

Pete moved from behind a tree and took out the enemy who hit Ritchie, then ducked.

"Take cover. There's still one left," Joey said.

"He's approaching from the south," Tony said. "I'm gonna let him get closer before I shoot. Stay hidden."

The enemy crawled on his belly through the woods. Before he reached the edge, he fired at Ritchie and hit him in the shoulder. Ritchie dropped his weapon and fell to the ground.

"Son of a bitch. I need help."

Tony focused his scope, and when the target moved forward, he took his shot.

"Headshot. That clears them out."

The GhostWalkers removed their headsets and turned the system off. Joey picked up his vape.

"How's that, Pete?" Tony asked.

"You got lucky."

"Whatever."

Tony paused. "Christ, did you hear Ritchie wail when he got hit? You would have thought it was a real bullet."

"Wait till it's you, Tony. It goddamn hurts. It's worse than when my dad gets drunk and beats me with a willow stick," Ritchie said.

"I'm with Ritchie. I knelt on a small rock and it hurt like hell," Pete said.

"All right, y'all, enough crying. We scored a win tonight, but we need to get better. We got two more wins to go."

"Don't worry, Joey. We'll get better," Pete said, then he and Ritchie opened the door and left.

"See you tomorrow."

"See y'all at school."

Chapter Fifteen
THE MCGILL RESIDENCE

Ritchie unlocked the door of a small ranch house, slipped inside, and stepped quietly toward his room.

A slurred voice came from the living room. "That you, boy?"

Ritchie froze at the sound. He looked into the kitchen and saw empty bottles on the counter. "Yeah, Dad, it's me. I just came from practice," he said quietly.

Ritchie's father stumbled into view, a drink in his hand, and his eyes unfocused.

"What'd I tell you about wastin' time with them games?"

"I'm not wastin' time. We could win big money."

His father gave a derisive laugh. "You really believe that shit?"

"It was on Facebook. It was even on the news."

His father took a long swig from his bottle and sneered. "You're so stupid it hurts."

"At least I'm not a drunk."

His father moved toward Ritchie, hand raised.

Ritchie instinctively backed away, then quickly ducked into his bedroom and locked the door. "Keep it up, old man. I'll show you."

Ritchie's room was a stark contrast to the rest of the house. It was meticulously clean and had gaming posters hanging on the walls.

He pulled out his controller, put on headphones, and put the volume on high to drown out the banging on his door.

The banging continued for another minute, then stopped. Heavy footsteps retreated down the hallway. A door slammed and the house fell silent except for the muffled sound of the television in the living room.

Ritchie sat on the edge of his bed, the controller gripped tight in his hands. His heart still pounded from the confrontation. He took several deep breaths and tried to calm himself.

This was the third night this week his father had come home drunk. The pattern was always the same: stumble in around nine or ten, start drinking what was left in the fridge, and find something to complain about. Most nights Ritchie avoided him by staying in his room. Tonight he stayed too late at Joey's.

He powered on his gaming system and logged into the practice server. The screen lit up with the main menu. A notification popped up showing Joey and Tony were online.

Ritchie clicked on the voice chat. "Hey, Dudes."

"There you are," Joey said. "We thought you bailed on us."

"Just got home late."

"Your old man giving you grief again?" Tony asked.

Ritchie didn't answer right away. He navigated through the menu and selected Piney Woods.

"I'm fine," he said. "Let's just run the scenario."

"You sure?" Joey asked.

"I'm sure. Let's go."

The game loaded and Ritchie's avatar materialized in the forest. He moved through the trees automatically, his mind only half focused on the screen. The other half kept replaying the look on his father's face, the raised hand, the sneering voice. *You're so stupid it hurts.*

Ritchie clenched his jaw and forced himself to concentrate. He positioned his avatar behind a fallen log and scanned the area for enemies.

"Ritchie, you got eyes on the eastern approach?" Joey asked.

"Yeah, I got it."

"You don't sound like you got it."

"I *said* I got it."

Joey went quiet for a moment. "All right. Stay sharp."

Ritchie watched the screen, waiting for movement. The forest was dense with fog, and visibility was poor. He adjusted his scope and swept from left to right.

An enemy appeared between the trees, moving cautiously toward the teleport station. Ritchie tracked the target and fired. The shot hit the soldier in the shoulder, dropping him.

"Nice shot," Tony said.

Ritchie didn't respond. He reloaded and repositioned behind a boulder. Another enemy came into view, this one more careful, using the trees for cover. Ritchie waited until the target paused to check his surroundings, then he fired. Headshot. The enemy went down.

"Two down," Ritchie said.

"You're on fire tonight," Joey said.

"I'm just doing my job."

They played for another hour, running the scenario three more times. Ritchie took out more enemies than anyone else on the team. His shots were precise, his movements efficient. He didn't waste ammunition or make careless mistakes.

When they finally logged off, Joey sent a private message: You good?

Ritchie stared at the screen. He typed: Yeah, and hit send.

He set the controller down and pulled off his headphones. The house was quiet now. His father had probably passed out on the couch or made it to his bedroom. Either way, the danger was gone for tonight.

Ritchie stood and walked to his desk. A college brochure from the University of Houston sat on top of a stack of notebooks. He picked it up from the guidance counselor's office last week. The tuition costs were listed on the back page: eleven thousand dollars per year for in-state students, but that didn't include books or the cost for the dorm.

He did the math in his head. The tournament prize was twenty-five thousand dollars, split four ways. That was six thousand two hundred and fifty dollars each. *Not enough for a full year, but enough for a semester, and if he got a part-time job ...*

It would be a start.

He opened the desk drawer and pulled out a notebook. Inside were pages of notes about the tournament that Tony had made and copied for each member: team strategies, WolfDen's patterns, maps of each scenario with marked positions and routes. Tony had spent hours looking for weaknesses and planning counter-strategies.

Ritchie flipped to a blank page and wrote: Three days until tournament, then he underlined it twice.

He closed the notebook and returned it to the drawer. The college brochure went back on top of the stack.

Ritchie changed into sweatpants and a t-shirt and climbed into bed. The sheets were clean. He had washed them himself that morning because his father never did laundry. The room smelled faintly of detergent and fresh air from the open window.

He lay in the dark and stared at the ceiling. Down the hall, his father snored which meant he was asleep for the night.

Ritchie closed his eyes and tried to sleep, but his mind raced. *What if Dad's right, and I really am stupid for believing this can work?*

The next morning, Ritchie woke to sunlight streaming through the window. He checked his phone: seven-thirty.

He dressed quickly and grabbed his backpack, then moved quietly through the house, stepping over empty beer cans in the hallway and avoiding the creaky floorboard near the kitchen.

The front door opened without a sound, and he stepped outside into the cool morning air. He pulled the door closed behind him and started walking toward Joey's house.

His phone buzzed. A text from Joey: Practice at noon. Don't be late.

Ritchie typed back: I'll be there.

He put the phone in his pocket and kept walking. The neighborhood was quiet. A few cars drove past, and a dog barked in someone's yard. Normal people were doing normal things, living normal lives.

Chapter Sixteen
CYPRESS HIGH SCHOOL

Pete strutted down a hall crowded with kids while rap music blared from his headsets. He nodded to his friends and fist-bumped them as he moved to the beat.

Shorty, a beanpole thin seventeen-year-old with a Chicago accent, rounded the corner and shot Pete a shit-eating grin. "What's up, dude? Worried about the next game?"

"Not if you're the competition."

Shorty brushed him off. "Keep thinkin' that, Moritz. I'll let you know how that trophy feels."

Pete turned the corner into a hallway lined with lockers. The banter of dozens of kids echoed off the walls, and the metallic crack of locker doors slamming shut filled the air.

Pete went to the third locker on the left, exchanged a few books, then closed the locker and ran to catch up with Joey. "I just saw Shorty, and he seemed overly confident."

"He's got a right to be. I watched them practice, and they got this new member named Brie. She's pretty damn good. She can be a sniper, a trooper, or a stalker."

"Are you saying she's good, or hot?"

Joey stepped beside Pete and pushed him. "Christ, Pete, you can't tell that from her avatar."

Pete grinned, his smile spreading his cheeks wide. "Are you trying to tell me you don't know who she is?"

Joey doubled over laughing, then he held his hands up in surrender. "All right. Maybe she's good *and* hot."

Pete walked closer to Joey and whispered, "Bullshit aside, you think she could replace Ritchie?"

Joey turned sharply, his eyes narrowing.

"I'm not ditching Ritchie yet. But we'll keep her in mind."

Joey paused. "Meanwhile, let's watch Shorty's team compete, and see if they've got anything to feel pumped about."

Pete laughed. "You just want to watch Brie again."

That night, Team GhostWalkers watched Shorty and his team in Joey's bedroom.

The monitor showed an unknown team going through the Urban Sprawl scenario, stealthily moving from one location to another and seldom exposing themselves. Pete sat up and pointed to the soldier on the right side of the screen.

"That's Shorty in the lead spot."

"And here comes Brie. She's getting in position as the sniper."

Tony got up and opened the door. "I'm grabbing a snack. Call me if anything good happens."

"Don't be long. I want to see what you think of this team."

"I already checked them out. Without Brie, Shorty's team is nothing."

Tony disappeared into the hallway. Joey grabbed the remote and turned up the volume. The sound of gunfire and footsteps filled the room.

On screen, Brie's avatar climbed a fire escape and positioned herself on a rooftop overlooking the main street. She went prone and scoped the area below.

"Look at her positioning," Ritchie said. "She's got sight lines on three different approach routes."

Pete leaned forward on his beanbag. "Shorty's moving up the western alley."

They watched as Shorty's avatar advanced through a narrow passage between two buildings. He moved cautiously, checking corners, and using dumpsters and debris for cover.

An enemy soldier appeared on a balcony across the street. Brie tracked his movement and fired. The target dropped.

"Damn," Joey said. "She didn't hesitate."

"Look at the kill-cam," Ritchie said.

The replay showed Brie's shot in slow motion. Headshot. Clean and precise. The bullet traveled through fog and hit the target between the eyes.

Tony came back into the room carrying a bag of chips. He sat down on his beanbag and stuffed a handful into his mouth.

"What did I miss?"

"Brie just made a hell of a shot," Pete said.

Tony watched the screen. Brie relocated to a different rooftop, moving quickly but staying low. She found a new vantage point and resumed scanning.

"She knows how to reposition," Tony said. "Most snipers stay in one spot too long."

Shorty's team advanced deeper into the urban sprawl. Two of his teammates flanked from opposite sides while Shorty pushed straight through the middle. Brie covered all three from above.

The enemy team tried to counter. Three soldiers rushed Shorty's position from the south. Brie tracked the first one and fired. She scored a hit, then shifted and fired again. Another hit. The third soldier ducked behind a burned-out car.

"Two down in three seconds," Ritchie said. "That's impressive."

Shorty's teammates closed in on the remaining enemy. They coordinated their approach, one drawing fire while the other flanked. The enemy went down in a crossfire.

"They're working together," Joey said. "That's what we need to do better."

The match continued for another ten minutes. Shorty's team

moved through the sprawl systematically, clearing sectors, controlling key positions. Brie provided overwatch the entire time, taking out enemies before they could engage Shorty's ground team.

When the victory screen appeared, Pete let out a low whistle. "They didn't lose a single player."

"Perfect run," Ritchie said.

Tony set down his chips and crossed his arms. "Run it back. I want to see it again."

Joey rewound the footage to the beginning. They watched it a second time, this time paying closer attention to the details. Tony called out observations as they went. "Watch how Brie communicates. She's giving them constant updates. Distance, direction, and threat level."

"And look at Shorty," Ritchie said. "He trusts her completely. He doesn't even check his six because he knows she's got it covered."

They watched Brie make another kill shot, this one at extreme range through a broken window.

"How did she even see that guy?" Pete asked.

"Movement," Tony said. "See how the curtain shifted? She picked up on it."

Joey paused the playback and looked at his team. "So what do you think?"

"She's good," Ritchie said. "Really good."

"Better than you?" Joey asked Tony.

Tony considered the question. "Different. I'm better at long range in open or wooded terrain. She's better at urban environments with multiple sight lines."

"Could she replace any of us?" Joey asked.

The room went quiet. Pete shifted on his beanbag while Ritchie stared at the floor.

"She could replace Ritchie," Pete said finally.

Ritchie's head snapped up. "The hell she could."

"You saw the same match I did. She's more versatile. She can snipe, but she can also move and reposition. You're good at one thing."

"One thing that wins matches," Ritchie said.

"When it works," Pete said. "But what happens when it doesn't?"

Joey raised his hand. "All right, enough. We're not making any decisions right now."

"But we should think about it," Pete said. "If Shorty's team dropped out, Brie's available. We'd be stupid not to consider it."

Tony reached for his chips again. "The tournament's in three days. Changing the roster now would be a mistake. We don't have time to build chemistry with someone new."

"Tony's right," Joey said. "We stick with what we have. If something changes, we'll deal with it then."

Ritchie stood up and walked to the window. He looked out at the street, his jaw tight. "I'm not getting replaced," he said.

"Nobody's replacing anybody," Joey said. "We're a team."

"For now," Pete muttered.

Joey shot him a look. "Drop it, Pete."

The tension in the room was thick. Tony ate his chips and pretended not to notice. Ritchie stayed at the window, his back to the others.

Joey grabbed the remote and started a new video. "Let's watch WolfDen's last match. That's who we're actually playing against."

The screen loaded, showing the Piney Woods scenario. WolfDen's team appeared at the northern spawn point.

"Here we go," Joey said.

They watched as WolfDen moved through the forest with military precision. No wasted movement, no unnecessary communication. They advanced as a unit, covering each other, anticipating threats.

"They move like they've done this before," Tony said. "Like it's real."

"It *is* real to them," Joey said. "That's the difference."

WolfDen reached the teleport station in under two minutes. They secured it and held it against three different enemy attacks. When the match ended, they had zero deaths and maximum kills.

Pete let out a long breath. "We're in trouble."

"Maybe," Joey said. "But we've beaten good teams before."

"Not like this," Ritchie said from the window. He turned to face the group. "They're on a different level."

Tony nodded slowly. "He's right. But that doesn't mean we can't beat them. We just have to be smarter."

"How?" Pete asked.

"By doing what they don't expect," Tony said. "They're used to teams that play conventionally. We need to break the pattern."

Joey leaned back on the sofa. "You got something in mind?"

"Maybe," Tony said. "Let me think about it."

The room fell silent again, but this time it was a different kind of silence. Not tension, but focus. They had seen the competition. They knew what they were up against.

Joey looked at each of them in turn. Pete on the beanbag, still watching the screen. Ritchie at the window, arms crossed. Tony eating chips, his eyes distant.

"We've got three days," Joey said. "We practice every night until the tournament. No excuses, no distractions. We give this everything we've got."

"And if we lose?" Pete asked.

"We won't," Joey said.

But even as he said it, he wasn't sure he believed it.

That night, after Pete and Ritchie had gone home, Tony stayed behind. He sat on the beanbag, controller in hand, running the Piney Woods scenario solo.

Joey came back into the room carrying two energy drinks. He tossed one to Tony and sat down on the sofa.

"You really think we can beat them?" Joey asked.

Tony didn't answer right away. He navigated his avatar through the forest, checking corners, scanning for threats.

"I don't know," he said finally. "They're better than anyone we've faced."

"But?"

"But they have patterns. Everyone has patterns." Tony paused the game and looked at Joey. "I just need to figure out what theirs are."

"And if you can't?"

Tony turned back to the screen. "Then we lose. And Ritchie

doesn't go to college. And Pete doesn't prove anything to his dad. And you don't get to tell everyone you won."

"And you?" Joey asked.

Tony restarted the game. "I just want to win."

Joey drank his energy drink and watched his brother play. Tony moved through the scenario with absolute focus, every movement calculated, every decision deliberate.

"You think we should get Brie?" Joey asked.

"Not now. Maybe after, or if we need a fifth for the next tournament."

"And Ritchie?"

Tony shrugged. "Ritchie's solid. But Pete's right. We need versatility."

Joey crushed his empty can and tossed it toward the trash. It bounced off the rim and hit the floor.

"Three days," he said.

"Three days," Tony repeated.

On the screen, Tony's avatar reached the teleport station. He stopped and studied it, examining every detail, and every angle of approach.

Somewhere in Damascus, WolfDen was doing the same thing.

The tournament was coming.

And only one team could win.

Chapter Seventeen
KAFEH SUPREME

Damascus

Rizwan entered the café and took his seat in front of the gaming system. Sandof and Shaklam followed closely behind him.

Cyrus sat in the corner as usual, a sour look on his face.

"Don't look so grim, Cyrus. No one has beaten us in Desert Sands, and only a few in the other scenarios."

Cyrus pounded his fist on the table and glared.

"Desert Sands doesn't matter. Urban Sprawl doesn't matter. The only one that matters is Piney Woods — where the teleportation point is. If we can't control that, we have nothing."

Cyrus glared at all of them, one at a time. "We will play that scenario every chance we get, until we can't be beaten. Understood?"

He waited for acknowledgement from all of them. "And don't forget, we're down two to one. We *need* to get to games six and seven. Nothing else matters."

Cyrus lowered his voice. "Drink your coffee, then we'll go upstairs and practice."

Cyrus sat in the corner of the cramped room above the Kafeh Supreme, his eyes locked on the gaming system. The afternoon sun filtered through the bullet-riddled walls, casting broken patterns across the concrete floor. He inhaled the scent of coffee drifting up from below, and the familiar aroma steadied his nerves.

Rizwan entered first, his footsteps heavy on the stairs. He dropped his bag on the floor and took his position at the second console. Sandof followed, removing his shoes at the doorway before crossing to his station. Shaklam arrived last, his fingers already drumming against his thigh.

"We have three practice matches today," Cyrus said. "All in Piney Woods."

Rizwan pulled his headset over his ears and adjusted the microphone. "Against who?"

"The first match is against the Brazilians. The second is the Korean team. And the third is whoever accepts the challenge."

Sandof powered on his system and watched the login screen materialize. The DNA scanner hummed as he placed his hand on the reader. "The Koreans are good."

"Everyone is good at this level." Cyrus turned to face the team. "But we need to be better. We need to control that teleportation point, or we have nothing."

Shaklam stopped his drumming and met Cyrus's gaze. "We beat the Brazilians twice already."

"Then we need to beat them a third time." Cyrus pulled on his haptic suit, and the sensors activated with a soft vibration. "The teleport station is our advantage. We know how to use it better than anyone. But it's only an advantage if we reach it first and hold it."

The team suited up in silence, each man checking his equipment, adjusting the fit of the sensors. Cyrus pulled his headset into place and selected the Piney Woods scenario.

Dense pine trees stretched in every direction, their trunks packed so close that movement required careful navigation. Morning fog hung between the branches, reducing visibility to thirty meters. Pine needles carpeted the ground, muffling footsteps but making it impossible to move without creating *some* sound.

Cyrus spawned at the northern edge of the map. He crouched low and scanned the terrain. The teleportation station sat in a small clearing two hundred meters southeast, inside a weathered wooden shack with a rusted metal roof.

"Positions," he whispered into the headset.

"West flank," Rizwan said.

"South approach," Sandof said.

"Rear guard," Shaklam said.

Cyrus moved through the trees, his rifle held at the ready. Every few steps he stopped to listen. The Brazilians would spawn somewhere south, and they would come fast, trying to claim the shack before WolfDen could establish control.

A branch snapped to his right. Cyrus froze and raised his weapon. Through the fog, he saw movement, a shadow weaving between the pines. He sighted the target and squeezed the trigger. The suppressed rifle made a soft sound, and the Brazilian soldier dropped.

"One down, northeast sector," Cyrus said.

"I've got eyes on the shack," Rizwan said. "Two hostiles approaching from the south."

"Take them."

Two muted shots echoed through the trees. Cyrus heard Rizwan's confirmation, and he advanced toward the clearing. The shack came into view through the fog, its walls weathered and cracked, its door hanging crooked on rusted hinges.

Sandof emerged from the south, moving in a low crouch. He reached the shack first and slipped inside. "Station secured."

"Shaklam, teleport to the rear and watch our backs," Cyrus said. "The last two are still out there."

Inside the shack, Shaklam looked at the teleport options: waterfalls, southern edge of lake, border with Urban Sprawl, and more.

He ignored all of them and entered the GPS coordinates he had, then pressed the activation button. The world blurred, and he materialized three hundred meters west, behind a massive boulder. He scanned the area through his scope and spotted the remaining Brazilians advancing through a dense stand of pines.

"Got them," Shaklam said. "West sector, moving your direction."

Cyrus positioned himself behind a fallen tree trunk. Rizwan moved to the opposite side of the clearing, creating a crossfire. The Brazilians came through the fog, their weapons sweeping left and right.

Cyrus waited until they were fifteen meters from the shack, then he opened fire. Rizwan fired simultaneously from the opposite angle. Both targets went down before they could return a shot.

The victory notification scrolled across Cyrus's visor: MATCH COMPLETE. WOLFDEN WINS.

Cyrus removed his headset and looked at the team. "Good. But we were too slow reaching the station. Next match, we move faster."

The Korean team spawned hard and fast. Cyrus barely had time to establish his position before enemy fire erupted from multiple angles. A round struck his shoulder, and the haptic suit delivered a sharp jolt of pain. He gritted his teeth and dropped behind cover.

"They're everywhere," Sandof said.

Cyrus peered around the tree trunk and spotted three Korean soldiers advancing in a wedge formation. They moved with precision, covering each other's movements, communicating in rapid bursts.

"Rizwan, flank right. Shaklam, get to the station and teleport behind them."

Rizwan broke from cover and sprinted through the trees. Bullets chewed into the bark around him, and splinters flew through the air. He dove behind a cluster of boulders and returned fire, forcing the Koreans to take cover.

Shaklam reached the shack and activated the teleport. He reappeared two hundred meters south, directly behind the Korean position. He took aim on the nearest soldier and fired twice. The target collapsed.

The Koreans reacted instantly, spinning to face the new threat.

Shaklam retreated behind a massive pine and reloaded. Bullets hammered into the tree, and chunks of bark exploded around him.

Cyrus used the distraction to advance. He moved quickly, covering ten meters with several long strides, and stopping behind trees to catch his breath. When he got within firing range, he sighted the Korean leader and squeezed the trigger. The shot took the man in the chest, and he went down.

The remaining Koreans fell back, regrouping near a rocky outcrop. Sandof advanced from the west, his assault rifle chattering in controlled bursts. One Korean went down.

The last Korean made a desperate run for the teleport station. Cyrus tracked him and fired. The bullet caught him mid-stride, and he collapsed ten meters from the shack.

MATCH COMPLETE. WOLFDEN WINS.

Cyrus pulled off his headset and wiped sweat from his forehead. His shoulder still ached from the earlier hit. "Better. We held the station. But they nearly flanked us."

Rizwan rubbed his arm where a simulated bullet had struck. "They were faster than the Brazilians."

"Everyone at this level is fast." Cyrus stood and stretched. "We need to be faster. And we need to anticipate their movements."

Shaklam poured water from a bottle and drank deeply. "One more match?"

"One more," Cyrus said. "Whoever accepts the challenge."

The third match came from an American team called the Razorbacks. They spawned with aggression, pushing hard from the south, firing as they advanced. Cyrus heard the gunfire before he saw them, a sustained barrage that tore through the forest.

"They're not being cautious," Sandof said.

"Good," Cyrus said. "Overconfidence gets you killed."

He moved to intercept, keeping low, and using the terrain for cover. Through the fog, he saw the Razorbacks advancing in a loose formation, their weapons firing at shadows. They wasted ammunition on phantom targets, shooting at movements that didn't exist.

Cyrus waited behind a thick pine trunk, his breathing steady, his finger resting lightly on the trigger. The first Razorback came within ten meters. Cyrus stepped out and fired three times. The target went down hard.

The other Razorbacks scattered, diving for cover. Cyrus ducked back behind the tree as return fire shredded the bark. Splinters struck his face, and the haptic suit registered minor impacts.

"Shaklam, get to the station," Cyrus said.

Shaklam sprinted through the trees, his boots kicking up pine needles. Bullets whipped past him, and one struck his leg. The haptic suit delivered a burst of pain, and he stumbled but kept moving. He reached the shack and dove through the doorway.

"Station secured," Shaklam said, breathing hard.

Rizwan engaged two Razorbacks near the eastern edge of the clearing. He fired in controlled bursts, forcing them to keep their heads down. One tried to rush his position, and Rizwan dropped him with a headshot.

Sandof circled wide, coming at the Razorbacks from an unexpected angle. He caught one reloading and put two rounds in his back. The man went down without firing a shot.

The last Razorback made a run for the teleport station. Shaklam stepped out of the shack and fired. The shot caught the runner in the side, spinning him around. He collapsed five meters from the door.

MATCH COMPLETE. WOLFDEN WINS.

Cyrus removed his headset and set it on the table. The room fell silent except for the sound of their breathing and the distant noise of traffic from the street below.

"Three wins," Rizwan said.

Cyrus nodded but didn't smile. "Three practice wins. The real matches start soon."

Sandof peeled off his haptic suit and rolled his shoulders. "We're ready."

"We're better," Cyrus said. "But ready is different. The GhostWalkers will be harder than any of these teams. They have that kid who never misses. The one who sees patterns."

Shaklam stretched his leg where the simulated bullet had struck. Even through the suit, the pain lingered. "We beat them in the last practice match."

"We surprised them," Cyrus said. "Next time, they'll be ready for our tactics. We need new ones."

Rizwan stood and moved to the window, looking at the street below. People moved through the market, buying vegetables and bread, living their lives as if the world wasn't about to change. "What if we don't control the teleport station?"

"We *will* control it," Cyrus said, and his voice carried the weight of absolute certainty. "Because we have to. Everything depends on it."

He looked at each member of the team in turn. Rizwan, who had lost his cousin to an airstrike. Sandof, whose sister was now a widow raising orphans. Shaklam, barely twenty-two, old enough to remember life before the war but too young to have known real peace.

"We train again tomorrow," Cyrus said. "Same scenario. Same station. We hold that position until we can do it in our sleep."

The team gathered their equipment in silence. Cyrus remained at the window, watching the sun sink toward the horizon, casting long shadows across Damascus.

"We will train because the GhostWalkers are training. We can't afford to ease up."

"They're kids!" Rizwan said. "We can —"

"I have watched them practice," Cyrus said. "The sniper they have is uncanny. I've seen him make shots that should have been impossible. So don't tell me they're just kids."

Chapter Eighteen
THE GHOSTWALKERS PRACTICE

Sean fixed coffee and was about to sit down when he heard a noise coming from Joey's bedroom. He set the cup down and went to see what it was.

The noise grew louder as he approached the door: shouting, cursing, and the sound of controllers clicking rapidly. Sean pushed the door open without knocking.

Joey sat on the worn sofa, a controller gripped tight in both hands. Pete and Ritchie were sprawled on beanbags in front of the big-screen TV, and Tony occupied the third beanbag, his headphones hanging around his neck.

Energy drink cans littered the floor around them, and the stale smell of vape smoke hung in the air despite the open window.

The TV screen showed the Piney Woods scenario. Their avatars moved through dense pine trees, weapons raised, scanning for enemies. Pete's character took a hit and stumbled backward.

"Goddamn it," Pete shouted. "Where did that come from?"

"Behind the boulder," Tony said, his voice calm. "Eleven o'clock."

Joey maneuvered his character to flank the position while Ritchie provided covering fire. The sound effects from the game filled the room: gunshots, footsteps crunching pine needles, the rustling of branches.

"What's going on?" Sean said, raising his voice to be heard over the noise. "Why are you guys here instead of at school?"

Joey didn't look away from the screen. He leaned forward, his thumbs working the controller. "There's no school today, Dad. It's Martin Luther King Day or something."

Sean's jaw tightened. "Or something? He's a man to be admired, and not just because you get a day off from school."

Joey turned to face his father. The other boys shifted uncomfortably on their beanbags. "Okay, Dad. Got it. Just let us finish the game."

Sean sighed and shook his head. He looked at each of the boys in turn, then back at Joey. "Listen, we've got a situation at work, and I have to go in. Make sure you help your mother with whatever she needs."

"Got it, Dad: Help mom."

Sean lingered in the doorway for a moment, watching them. They sat frozen, waiting for him to leave. He turned and walked down the hallway.

Joey waited until he heard the front door close, then he focused on the game again. "He pisses me off sometimes."

"Dad's just being dad," Tony said, adjusting his headphones.

"He didn't have to interfere with our game. He knows how important it is." Joey took a long drink from his energy drink and set the can down hard on the floor. "We've got two more matches before we face WolfDen."

Pete grabbed his controller and settled back into his beanbag. "Your dad's cool compared to mine. At least he doesn't think gaming is for kids."

"Yeah, well, he still treats us like we're ten years old." Joey repositioned himself on the sofa and cracked his knuckles. "All right, enough talk. Let's run it again."

Ritchie pointed at the screen. "We need a better strategy for holding the teleport station. WolfDen's gonna come at us hard."

"Tony can cover it from the ridge," Joey said. "Nobody gets past his sight line."

Tony shook his head. "I might miss them if they flank from the west. There's a lot of cover in that sector."

"Then we need someone watching the western approach," Pete said. "I'll take it."

Joey started the game, and their avatars materialized in the forest. The morning fog hung between the trees, reducing visibility and creating an eerie atmosphere.

They split up according to plan: Tony headed north to the high ground, Pete moved west, Ritchie advanced south, and Joey made his way toward the teleport station in the center.

The station sat inside a weathered wooden shack with a rusted metal roof. Joey reached it first and ducked inside. The teleport interface glowed on the screen, showing GPS coordinates and activation controls.

"Station secured," Joey said.

"I've got movement," Tony said, his voice quiet and focused. "Three hostiles, coming from the southeast."

Pete repositioned behind a fallen tree trunk. Ritchie crouched low and moved through the underbrush. Joey stayed in the shack, watching the door, his finger resting on the trigger.

The enemy team advanced through the fog while Tony tracked them through his scope, calculating distance and wind. He fired once, and the lead soldier dropped. The other two scattered, diving for cover.

"Nice shot," Ritchie said.

"Two left," Tony said. "Pete, you got eyes on them?"

"Negative," Pete said. "They went to ground."

Joey leaned closer to the screen, his jaw clenched. This was the critical moment. If they lost control of the station, they lost the match. If WolfDen could do this to them in the real tournament, they would lose everything.

A shadow moved between the trees on the western edge. Pete saw it and swung his rifle around, but the enemy was faster. A muzzle flash lit up the fog, and Pete's avatar jerked backward as bullets struck his chest.

"I'm hit," Pete said. "Damn it."

"Fall back to the station," Joey said. "Ritchie, cover him."

Ritchie fired blindly into the fog, forcing the enemy to take cover. Pete limped through the trees, his health bar dropping into the red. He reached the shack and stumbled through the doorway.

"I'm down to twenty percent," Pete said.

"Stay here," Joey said. "Tony, where's the other one?"

Tony scanned through his scope, moving slowly from left to right. The fog made it difficult to see more than thirty meters. He watched for movement, for anything out of place. A branch swayed near a cluster of boulders, but there was no wind.

"Got him," Tony said. "Behind the rocks, forty meters northeast."

The enemy soldier broke from cover and sprinted toward the shack. Tony tracked the movement and fired. The shot hit the runner in the shoulder, spinning him around, but he kept moving. Tony fired again, and this time the target went down.

"Last hostile eliminated," Tony said.

The victory notification scrolled across the screen: MATCH COMPLETE. GHOSTWALKERS WIN.

Joey set his controller down and leaned back against the sofa. "That was too close."

"They almost flanked us," Ritchie said.

Pete shook his head and rubbed his eyes. "I should have seen him coming. I wasn't paying attention."

"You held the western approach long enough," Joey said. "That's what matters."

Tony removed his headphones and set them on the floor. "WolfDen won't make those mistakes. They'll coordinate better. They'll use the teleport to get behind us."

"That's *if* they get the teleport station, which means we need to control it from the start," Joey said. "No matter what."

Ritchie stood and stretched, his back cracking. "How many practice matches have we done today?"

"Four," Joey said. "We won three."

"We need to win them all," Tony said. "Against WolfDen, three out of four won't cut it, because I guarantee, they'll win the Desert Sands, and probably the Urban Sprawl."

Pete grabbed another energy drink from the floor and popped the tab. The carbonation hissed as he took a long drink. "You think they're practicing now?"

"Probably," Joey said. "They're as serious about this as we are."

"More serious," Tony said. "They've got something to prove."

Joey looked at his Tony. "What do you mean?"

Tony picked up his controller and turned it over in his hands. "I watched some of their matches online. They don't play like it's a game. They play like it's personal."

"It *is* personal," Ritchie said. "Twenty-five thousand dollars is personal."

"It's more than that," Tony said. "The way they move, the way they coordinate. It's like they've done this before."

Pete laughed. "Done what? Played video games? We've all done that."

"No," Tony said. "I mean the real thing. I'm sure they've been in combat."

The room fell silent. Joey set his energy drink down and stared at the TV screen. The victory notification had faded, replaced by the main menu.

"You think they're military?" Joey said.

"Maybe," Tony said. "Or something like it."

Ritchie sat on his beanbag. "How can you tell?"

"Patterns," Tony said. "They don't waste movements and they don't panic when things go wrong. — they simply adapt."

"So do we," Pete said.

"Not the same way," Tony said. "When we mess up, we get frustrated. When they mess up, they adjust quickly and keep going."

Joey picked up his controller. "Then we need to learn to do the same thing."

"We've only got a couple of days," Ritchie said. "That's not a lot of time."

"It's enough," Joey said. "We run the scenario until we can do it without thinking."

Pete groaned and slumped deeper into his beanbag. "How many more times?"

"As many as it takes," Joey said.

Tony pulled his headphones back on and settled into position. Ritchie grabbed his controller and shifted forward on the beanbag. Pete drained the rest of his energy drink and crushed the can in his fist.

Joey started a new match.

Four hours later, afternoon sunlight streamed through the window.

Empty energy drink cans formed a pyramid in the corner of the room, and the smell of vape smoke had dissipated, replaced by the stale odor of teenage sweat and junk food.

Joey's mother knocked on the door and pushed it open without waiting for a response. She stood in the doorway, hands on her hips, surveying the mess.

"How long have you boys been at this?" she asked.

Joey spoke without taking his eyes off the screen. "Since this morning."

"It's almost three o'clock. Have any of you eaten?"

The boys looked at each other. None of them had thought about food.

"I'll take that as a no," she said. "I'm making sandwiches. Come eat."

"We're in the middle of a match," Joey said.

"The match will be there in twenty minutes. Come eat."

She left the door open and walked back toward the kitchen. Joey sighed but then forced a pause — one of two he was allowed — and set his controller down. The others did the same.

They filed out of the bedroom and down the hallway to the

kitchen. The table was set with plates and glasses of water. A tray of sandwiches sat in the center: ham and cheese, turkey, roast beef.

The boys grabbed sandwiches and ate in silence. Joey's mother watched them from the counter, her arms crossed. "Your father said you have a big tournament coming up."

Joey nodded, his mouth full.

"Is it important?"

Joey swallowed. "Very."

"Important enough to skip lunch?"

"We didn't have time."

She poured herself a cup of coffee and leaned against the counter. "What happens if you win?"

"We get twenty-five thousand dollars," Pete said. "Split four ways."

"And new gaming systems," Ritchie added.

"And a movie deal," Tony said.

Joey's mother raised her eyebrows. "A movie deal?"

"About the tournament," Joey said. "And about us."

"That seems like a lot of pressure for a video game."

"It's not just a video game," Joey said. "It's the biggest tournament of the year. Teams from all over the world are competing."

She sipped her coffee and studied them. "Who are you playing against?"

"A team called WolfDen," Joey said. "And they're good."

"Very good," Tony said. "Maybe better than us."

"Then you'll have to be better than very good," she said.

Joey finished his sandwich and reached for another. "That's what we're trying to do, but *some* people keep interrupting us."

"Just don't forget to take care of yourselves while you're doing it. Your father and I didn't raise you to live on energy drinks and vape smoke."

"Yes, ma'am," Joey said.

The boys finished eating and carried their plates to the sink. Joey's mother stopped them before they could leave.

"One more thing," she said. "Whatever happens in this tournament, you boys remember that it's just a game. Don't let it become more important than it should be."

Joey nodded. "We won't."

But as they walked back to the bedroom, he knew that wasn't entirely true. It had already become more than a game. It was a chance to prove something, and win something that mattered. And they weren't going to let WolfDen take that away from them.

They settled back into their positions: Joey on the sofa, the others on the beanbags. Tony pulled his headphones on. Pete cracked his knuckles. Ritchie took a deep breath.

Joey started the next match.

On the screen, they materialized in the fog-shrouded forest of Piney Woods. The teleport station waited in the distance, and somewhere in the trees, an enemy team was spawning, ready to take it from them.

Bring it on, Tony thought. *We're ready.*

Chapter Nineteen
OFFICE OF THE F.B.I.

Sean sat at his desk with the door open. He held a warm mug of coffee as he powered on his computer, the hum of the machine blending with the bustling sounds of the office: people chatted, copiers whirred, phones rang, and file cabinets opened and slammed shut.

The phone rang and Sean answered. It was the director.

"That imminent threat I told you about has legs."

"How's that?"

"We intercepted an encrypted message and it said, 'after we finish with the GhostWalkers, we'll take care of the other target.'"

Daniels paused. "I'm certain the language they used was code for something, but we don't know what."

"They said GhostWalkers? You're sure?"

"Positive. Why?"

Sean paused and then laughed. "My kids played a video game, and their team name is GhostWalkers. From what I've seen, I wouldn't want to be against them."

Director Samuels chuckled. "They're good, huh?"

"So good that I think the Army should use the game for training, and use them as instructors."

Samuels laughed. "I'll consider that for us as well. In the meantime, keep a close watch on any potential threats."

As Sean opened the door, Samuels called to him. "And unless you've got reason to suspect your kids, I think we can presume the name is a coincidence."

Sean laughed. "I think we can bet on the coincidence part. Either way, I've advised my people to be on full alert. In fact, I just sent them a message before I came up here." Sean paused. "But I *will* watch my kids."

As Samuels left, Sean stared at a family picture sitting on his desk. His wife smiled from the center, flanked by their two teenagers. Both kids wore gaming headsets around their necks. The photo was from last summer, taken at the beach house before everything got complicated at work.

Sean picked up the frame and studied his son's face. He had gotten serious about gaming in the past year, spending hours each night with his team. Sean had dismissed it as typical teenage behavior, but now the coincidence bothered him.

He set the picture down and pulled up the encrypted message on his screen. The words stared back at him: GhostWalkers. He scrolled through the rest of the intelligence report, looking for any connection he might have missed.

His phone buzzed. A text from his Missy: Sean, what time will you be home. I'm cooking spaghetti.

Sean typed back: I'll make sure I'm home early for spaghetti. No later than six.

Chapter Twenty
IT'S ALL IN THE NAME

Sean knocked on Joey's door, waited, then stepped inside.

"Hey, Dad," Tony said.

Sean leaned down and tousled Tony's hair. "At work today, we had a lead on some terrorists who mentioned the GhostWalkers."

"Get outta here," Joey said.

"Bring 'em on and we'll give 'em an ass kicking," Ritchie said, then he blushed and covered his mouth. "Sorry, Mr. Lugullo."

Sean laughed. "No worry, Ritchie. If that's the worst that comes out of your mouth, I'll be happy." He paused. "I don't know why I stopped by, other than to say if you happen to hear anything about terrorist activity, let me know."

"You got it, Mr. Lugullo."

Sean left the room and Joey got on the floor with the others. "All right, listen up. We get one game to practice with WolfDen before the competition, so we need to make this count. And it'll be with the new suits so we'll get a sense for how they feel."

"What's the scenario gonna be?" Pete asked.

"Not sure. I'm guessing either Piney Woods or Urban Sprawl."

"I hope it's not Urban Sprawl," Tony said. "I've seen 'em play that one, and they're good — real good."

Joey and Tony walked slowly down the hall toward their classes, each carrying an armload of books.

Brie, 17 with an adorable smile and confidence to match, sneaked behind Joey and pushed his books to the ground.

Joey blurted out, "Goddamn! You son of a bitch," before he knew who did it.

Brie quickly reached to pick up the books. "It's no big deal, Joey. I just wanted to see if I could sneak up on you."

Embarrassed by his reaction, Joey hurriedly began to pick up the books as well.

They met, head to head as they bent over the books. Brie smiled. "I heard you were watching me play the other night."

"Who told you that?"

"Does it matter? I heard. That's all you need to know."

Joey gave it thought for a moment, then said, "Come by the house tonight, and you'll see what I can do. We're playing a practice game with WolfDen."

Joey smiles at her. "Who knows, you might even want to join the team once you see how good we are."

"I thought you had a team?"

"We need a fifth."

"Dream on if you think I'll be a backup."

"Whatever. You should still watch. But you need to be there by seven."

"I'll be there," Brie said. "But you better be good."

Joey laughed. "If you're measuring good by Shorty's performance, then I'll be better than good."

Brie stood and handed him the last book. "Shorty's not bad. He just needs better teammates."

"Is that right?"

"That's right." She turned and walked away, glancing back over her shoulder. "See you at seven."

Tony waited until she was out of earshot. "You really think she'll come?"

"She'll come." Joey shifted his books and started walking. "The question is whether she'll want to join after she sees us play."

"She's got an attitude."

"Yeah, but she's got skills too. You saw her the other night. She's better than Ritchie, maybe better than Pete."

Tony stopped walking. "You're serious about this."

"We need five for the tournament. You know that. A backup is mandatory."

"What if she says no?"

Joey shrugged. "Then we find someone else. But I don't think she'll say no."

At lunch, Joey sat with his team in the corner of the cafeteria. Ritchie had his laptop open, reviewing footage from their last practice session.

"Look at this," Ritchie said, turning the screen. "Right here, when we rushed the compound. Pete went left when he should've gone right."

Pete leaned in. "I was providing cover."

"You were out of position. If this had been WolfDen, they would've flanked us."

"He's right," Joey said. "We're too predictable. They've probably watched every match we've had."

"So what do we do?" Tony asked.

Joey pulled out a notebook and sketched a quick diagram. "We change our approach. Instead of the standard rush, we split into two teams. Tony and I go high, you go low. We force them to choose which group to engage."

"That leaves both groups vulnerable," Pete said.

"Only if we don't communicate. The new suits have better voice quality. We use that."

Ritchie closed his laptop. "What about the fifth player? You really think Brie's gonna join?"

"I saw her play. She's good. The question is whether she'll consider playing as a backup."

"Being 'good' isn't enough against WolfDen. We need someone who's great."

Joey met his eyes. "Then we make her great. We've got time."

"Five weeks isn't a lot of time," Tony said. "The tournament starts Seanh fifteenth."

"Five weeks then." Joey looked around the table. "Anyone got a better option?"

No one spoke.

"Then it's settled. She watches tonight, and if she's interested, we bring her in."

After school, Joey found Brie at her locker. She was sorting through a stack of textbooks, her backpack already stuffed.

"You still coming tonight?" Joey asked.

She didn't look up. "I said I would."

"Just checking."

"I don't say things I don't mean." She closed the locker and turned to face him. "What time did you say?"

"Seven."

"And this is a practice game?"

"Against WolfDen. They're ranked first in the region."

Brie raised an eyebrow. "You think you can beat them?"

"We'll find out tonight."

"What if you can't?"

"Then we learn from it and get better." Joey shifted his weight. "That's the point of practice."

She studied him for a moment. "You really want me on your team, don't you?"

"We need a fifth, and you're the best option."

"Best option? That's supposed to flatter me?"

Joey smiled. "You want me to lie and say you're the only option?"

"I want you to be honest."

"Fine. You're good, probably better than half my team. But you've got no experience playing coordinated team strategy. You're a solo player trying to carry four dead weights."

Brie's expression hardened. "Shorty's team isn't that bad."

"They're not that good either. And you know it, or you wouldn't have been watching me the other night."

"Who says I was watching you?"

"You were sitting in the back row of the gaming cafe. You stayed for ninety minutes and left right after we finished our session."

She crossed her arms. "Maybe I was just killing time."

"Maybe. Or maybe you were looking for a real team." Joey paused. "Either way, I'll see you at seven." He walked away before she could respond.

At home, Joey's mother was setting the table for dinner when he came through the door.

"How was school?" she asked.

"Fine."

She smiled. "Your father mentioned he talked to you last night about some work thing."

"The GhostWalkers name. Yeah, he told us."

"He's not worried, is he?"

Joey dropped his backpack by the stairs. "I don't think so. It's probably just a coincidence."

"Probably." His mother turned back to the kitchen. "Dinner's in twenty minutes. And your father said some of your friends are coming over tonight?"

"It's a practice game, so we need the house quiet for a few hours."

"How many friends?"

"Four, maybe five."

"Five?"

"We might have a new team member. She's coming to watch."

His mother's eyes lit up. "She?"

"Mom, don't start."

"I'm not starting anything. I think it's nice you're inviting a girl over."

"To play video games."

"That still counts." She grinned. "What's her name?"

"Brie."

"Pretty name. Is she nice?"

Joey headed for his room. "She's competitive, skilled, and has an attitude. That's all I know."

"She sounds perfect for you."

"What's that supposed to mean?"

"It means you finally found someone who won't let you win." She went back to the stove. "Dinner in twenty minutes. Don't be late."

Chapter Twenty-One
WATCHING THE GAME

Missy Lugullo pulled the door open, her eyes widening when she saw Brie on the doorstep. Her lips pressed into a thin line before curving into a polite, restrained smile. "You must be Brie. Let me show you to Joey's room."

Missy called out as she led Brie down the hallway. "Brie's here."

Joey panicked, quickly jumping up and ripping down the girl posters. He yelled in a whispered shout. "C'mon help me get these down."

As Pete removed the last poster, Brie and Missy entered, and carefully made their way across the floor, avoiding numerous empty cans and bottles as well as small trashcans.

"Don't mind the mess, Brie." Missy shot Joey a glare.

"Or the filth and stench."

Joey patted the sofa seat next to him. "Hey, everybody, this is Brie. And, Brie, this is Pete, Ritchie, and my brother, Tony."

Brie looked around the room, noticing the clean spots where the posters had been. "What was up there, Joey?"

Joey brushed his hand in the air. "Just some old posters."

Tony laughed. "Brie, he's a teenage boy."

Brie attempted to hide a giggle. "Enough said."

Tony put on his new headphones, and shot a thumbs up to Joey. "Thanks for the new gear, Bro."

Tony, Pete, and Ritchie sat on the beanbags, and Brie settled in on the sofa next to Joey. He put his arm over Brie's shoulder and gestured for her to come closer.

"All right, y'all, we need to kick ass tonight. This is a key practice, and it's against WolfDen."

Tony turned the game on, and after the team entered their DNA the screen flashed the location:

Missy looked in on them. "Is everything all right?"

"Mom, close the door," Tony said. "We're playing a game."

"I'll close it, but you better behave."

Tony quickly ran for the highest building carrying his sniper rifle while he reminded the others of the plan. "Don't forget your assignments: Joey, approach from the west, but do it carefully. Pete, come in from the east, and Ritchie from the south."

He paused. "And wait for my signal before advancing."

Once everyone got into position, Tony sent the signal through their headsets. "Go."

Joey sneaked around two buildings, headed west, then moved north along the wall, keeping to the shadows. A long string of garbage sat on the side of a road that headed east/west, and Joey followed it cautiously.

Pete mimicked Joey's approach, but he did it from the east.

Ritchie moved from the south and headed directly for the target, a location about two hundred yards north.

All the while, Tony scoped the territory with his sniper rifle, waiting for an enemy to show their head.

Ritchie moved slowly from behind a dumpster, but before he got ten feet, he was hit in the right arm.

"Goddamn. That hurt."

He ducked behind the dumpster, barely dodging another shot. "Tony, help me out. I'm pinned down in the alley west of you."

Tony crawled on his belly across the rooftop but was careful to stay below the parapet. By the time he reached the west side, two more enemies sneaked up behind Ritchie and shot him four or five times in the gut and chest.

"Goddamn. Goddamn. That's it. I quit."

He threw down his gun and raised his hands, but he wasn't dead yet, so the WolfDen soldiers took him to a holding cell for captured members.

Tony positioned himself near the edge and fired a shot, hitting one of the WolfDen team in the chest. Another quick shot took him out, but the others got away.

Tony rushed back to the front of the building but saw nothing.

"GH1, this is GH4. Ritchie's out. I got one of the WolfDen team, but no sign of the others. I'll keep a watch for them."

Joey moved very slowly through the piles of garbage, using the bigger items to hide behind. Just as he stepped out from behind a rusted-out car, one of WolfDen's team stabbed him in the gut and another one shot him and took him out.

Moments later, they did the same to Pete, leaving only Tony left. Before he could get off the roof, three WolfDen soldiers climbed the stairs and surrounded him. Tony looked from one to the other, but then set his gun down and raised his hands.

Tony took off his headset and headed toward the restroom. "That sucked."

"Tell me about it," Pete said. "Ritchie ruined everything."

Tony stopped before exiting the door. "Ritchie didn't ruin anything. We all got taken out, so face it, Pete, they kicked our ass. And badly."

"I still say it's Ritchie's fault."

Ritchie reached over and smacked Pete on the side of the head.

Pete jumped up and punched Ritchie, which started a fight. Ritchie tackled Pete to the ground, and then they rolled around punching each other.

Brie curled up and lay her head on Joey's lap. Then Joey leaned down and kissed her.

"They do this shit all the time, Brie."

The door burst open, and Missy Lugullo stood in the doorway glaring at Pete and Ritchie with her hands on her hips. "What in the world is going on? You two are supposed to be friends."

Pete and Ritchie stopped fighting immediately. Pete moved back to his chair and Ritchie got up to leave.

"Sorry, Mrs. Lugullo." Ritchie stormed out the door.

Missy glared at Joey and Brie, her eyes wide.

"Joey. In the kitchen. Now!"

Brie sat up and moved to the end of the sofa, and Joey followed his mother out the door.

"Be right back."

Joey stormed into the kitchen, but kept his voice to a whisper. "What was that all about? You looked at Brie like she was trash. Is it because she's black?"

Missy sat erect and gasped. "Of course, not! For God's sake, we've never felt that way."

"That's the way it seemed. The way you looked, and the way you talked."

Missy looked toward the bedroom, then back to Joey. "Take a seat."

She paced while glancing at Joey. "Remember your cousin Megan? Married at eighteen with a baby on the way. I don't want you in that situation."

"That won't happen. And somebody needs to tell Brie nothing was meant."

"Call her in here, and I'll do it right now."

Joey shook his head. "Never mind. I'll do it."

Pete looked at Joey when he walked in. "What about Brie?"

"We'll see."

Brie looked at Pete, then Joey. "I'm right here, you know."

Chapter Twenty-Two
A NEW MEMBER

The next night, Pete, Tony, and Joey sat, waiting to play. Pete glanced at the time, then turned to Joey. "You sure she's coming?"

"She said she'd be here."

The bedroom door opened, and Missy Lugullo stepped inside. She brushed her hand in the air wafting the smoke aside. "Are you boys smoking?"

"Smoking?" Pete asked.

Ritchie looked up. "Us?"

"Everybody smokes, Mom. Besides, it's only vapes."

"Well, I won't have it. Not even vapes."

Tony laughed. "You wouldn't want the alternative."

Missy stood with her hands on her hips. "Would you like me to sit and watch you play?"

Joey kicked Tony's leg. "We won't smoke, Mom. Promise."

"Sorry, Mom," Tony said.

Just then the doorbell rang. "I'll get it," Missy said.

She returned a moment later with Brie. "Joey, this young lady said you invited her over."

Joey's face lit up.

"Hey, Brie. How's it going?"

"I'm ready."

"Joey said you were good — are you?" Pete asked.

Brie laughed.

"Give me a shot, and I'll show you."

Brie sat on the sofa next to Joey, and the others sat in their beanbags on the floor.

"Hey, if anyone doesn't remember, this is Brie. She used to play for Shorty's team, but they dropped out."

"My team knew they couldn't win. Y'all don't have that problem."

"You think we can win?" Pete asked.

"Not with the team you have. But if you had me ..."

"Consider it done. We're letting Ritchie go," Joey bowed his head. "Actually, he quit."

"Make sure not to let him go permanently," Tony said. "He can serve as a backup."

"How much will we have to pay him?" Pete asked.

"The same as everyone else" Tony said. "He's been with us the whole time, so he deserves it."

"I agree," Brie said. "Let's not quibble over pennies until we win the prize."

"Brie's got it right. We concentrate on winning, then we decide how to split it up. Let's meet here tomorrow to practice. We've only got a few days before the tournament starts."

Joey closed the door and addressed the other team members. "Speaking of the tournament, I've got a proposition for a new strategy; actually, it's Tony's idea, but I agree with him."

"Don't leave us guessing," Brie said.

"We change it up and work with two snipers: Tony and Brie. Tony on the roof and Brie on the ground. Pete and I will do the flanking and the direct attacks."

"I don't like it," Pete said.

"What's not to like? In the last three games, Tony has taken out more enemies than the rest of us combined."

"I don't know. I just don't like it."

"Like it or not, that's the way it's going to be. Now, everyone focus. We start tomorrow night."

Brie and Pete showed up early and made their way to Joey's bedroom. Joey and Tony joined them, and they all got ready to fight.

"Listen up. We've got thirty seconds to get ready. Tony will be positioned high in the trees. Pete and I will advance from the west and south, and Brie will advance from the east, but she'll also act as a sniper."

"Let's do it," Tony said.

They turned the game on and entered their DNA. Afterward, the screen flashed the location: Piney Woods — night.

Joey tapped Brie's shoulder.

"Remember, you have to be invisible. You can't let them see you."

"I'm black, Joey. You don't have to worry about me being invisible at night. Your ass is covered."

Joey took a long circuitous route crossing creeks and backtracking his steps so he couldn't be followed.

Pete did the same from the east side, and Brie inched forward from the south, making sure to keep her head below the foliage.

From a perch high in a grandfather pine, Tony scouted the area. "Two approaching from the northeast. Stay low."

Joey hugged the ground tighter and stopped moving while keeping an eye on the enemy. Suddenly, the enemy appeared not five feet from him. He fired once and hit one of them in the chest, but before he could get off another shot, the second one shot him twice — fatal shots.

Brie moved forward, as quiet as a snake, and when she had the opportunity, she fired, hitting the enemy in the leg. He limped away while firing behind him.

Brie continued crawling through the forest, tracking the enemy who was wounded. She slowed when he stopped at an ammo shack and went inside. The shack wasn't big; no bigger than a small tool shed.

Brie waited patiently for him to come out and inched closer all the time. She was about to pull the trigger when he spoke into a comm device. She was close enough to hear the conversation.

"WolfDen III, this is WolfDen IV. Do you copy?"

"I'm here but injured. It's a leg shot, so not disqualifying."

"Did you get Richardson?"

"Negative. I never got the chance."

"Return to base immediately."

WolfDen III stepped into an adjacent structure that looked similar to an old phone booth, and he sat on a padded seat. He pushed buttons on a keypad, then disappeared.

Brie blinked and looked again, but he was gone. She sneaked up to the structure and inspected it, but nothing was there and there were no signs of any of the team members.

"What the hell?"

Brie approached the structure stealthily, and upon confirming no one was inside, she entered.

There was a small table with a monitor and a keyboard, and hanging on the wall was a small keypad with numbers only.

She pressed a few numbers but nothing happened. After trying a few more options, she moved away slowly. A low humming came from the monitor and Brie quickly took cover behind the shelter of nearby boulders.

She waited until there was no noise, then she crawled away and contacted the rest of the team.

"This is GH5 calling GH2. Meet me where we started but watch out. GH4, stay in your perch and keep your eyes open."

Brie made her way back to the entrance where they started and just before getting there, she met Tony and Pete.

"We've got to plan this out. I think we should stick together and attack all at once," Tony said.

"I'm with Tony on this," Pete said.

Brie was just about to answer when Tony tapped her on the shoulder. "Three soldiers coming up behind us."

They turned to face the oncoming soldiers but failed to notice a soldier approaching from the west. He slowed his approach, then when close enough, he fired and hit Pete in the back of the head.

He then fired again and hit Brie in the leg. She rolled over quickly and returned fire while Tony fended off the soldiers coming from the south.

Tony took out one, but the others escaped. Brie delivered a head-shot to the soldier who shot her, but when she turned to the south, the other two took her out, then they ducked for cover.

"The only one left is the sniper. Make your way north, and I'll stay here."

Tony surveilled the area, then slowly left his perch and began his descent. He didn't get four feet and a bullet hit the tree, inches from his head. He scooted back to the perch and stayed low. He pulled a high-powered flashlight from his pocket and shined it toward the soldier to the north. He then fired in that direction.

When the enemy shot at his light, he made a break for it on the east side of the tree. About ten feet down, he was hit: one to the chest and one to the head.

His character was removed from the game.

"Guess we screwed that up," Tony said.

Pete poked Tony's chest several times.

"The question is, how did they get behind us without you spotting them? That's part of what a sniper is supposed to do."

Joey stepped up and separated them. "For now, I just want to forget this day happened."

Joey removed his headset and lit a smoke, then he nudged Tony's back with his foot. "Now we can talk about how they got past you."

"Damned if I know. They must have had a tunnel or something because I watched the whole time and saw nothing."

"That's bullshit," Pete said.

"Hang on, Pete. We can't blame Tony. We all saw the WolfDen team on the north side of us when we started. If they got behind us, they must have moved far to the west or east and circled back."

Tony shook his head.

"I'd have seen them if they did."

Pete scoffed. "But you didn't see them, did you? There's no other way they could have gotten around us."

Brie squinted her eyes, staring at the wall.

"I'm not so sure. When I tracked one of them, he went into what appeared to be an old ammo shack. Then he called his leader and told him he was wounded." She paused. "The funny thing is the leader asked him if he got Rickson ... Richard ... Something like that, and the guy said he never got the chance."

"What the hell does that mean?" Joey asked.

"I don't know, but then he got into something that looked like an old phone booth, he tapped on what I later found out was a keypad, then he disappeared."

"Come on. You expect us to believe that shit?" Pete said.

"Believe it or not, that's what happened."

"Then what?" Joey asked.

Brie took a long swig from her water bottle.

"After he disappeared, I went to the ammo shack. Nobody was there, but there was a table with a monitor and keyboard, and on the wall was a small keypad with nothing but numbers."

"A keypad?"

"What kind of numbers?" Tony asked.

"I'm not sure, but there was an almost identical keypad in that booth."

"I think we need to go back there and have a closer look," Joey said.

"And how the hell do you think we can do that?" Pete asked.

"We're allowed two practice sessions between each tournament game. We can use one of them to check it out."

"I'm guessing it was one of those teleport spots I mentioned."

The GhostWalkers made their way to the ammo shack. Once there, they all went in different directions to ensure no one was around.

After surveilling the area, Brie got on the comm.

"GhostWalkers, this is GH5, all clear."

Tony, Joey, and Pete joined Brie, and they entered the ammo shack. It was the same as when Brie saw it before.

She moved quickly to the table.

"Here's the monitor I told you about."

Joey pointed to the numbers: 44° 58° 38°.28° N: -93° 15° 55.44° W

"So what's it all mean?" Pete asked.

Tony laughed.

"Christ, Pete, they're GPS coordinates."

"What?"

"GPS coordinates, asshole."

"Maybe we should enter a coordinate into the keypad," Brie said.

"Worth a try."

Tony stepped up to the keypad and was about to enter numbers, but then he stopped.

"I think we should know exactly where these coordinates will take us — if that's what they do — and I also think we should copy these coordinates in case things go wrong."

"Where are we gonna get coordinates, at least ones we know?" Joey asked.

"I know the coordinates for our house, so hang onto your ass."

"I think we should hold onto each other when we do this," Brie said.

They grabbed each other by the hand or arm and waited while Tony entered the data. When he was done, he hit enter and a loud whirring sound was heard, then they disappeared from where they were and ended up near another portal.

Brie looked at the monitor where they appeared.

"The coordinates are different."

"They're the ones I entered."

"Let's see what happens if we exit the portal," Pete said.

"I'm betting we'll exit at our house, but outside, near the street."

They looked at each other with a tinge of curiosity and fear. Joey stepped forward first, still grasping Brie's hand. "Let's do it."

They stepped onto the portal and pressed a green button on the keypad. Instantly, they were teleported to the front yard of Joey's house, near the street.

Pete stared, baffled, while Tony stood up and looked around. "Holy shit, it worked."

"I'll be damned."

"And if we go into the house, we won't be there," Tony said.

"So what the hell does that mean? And what are those people planning?" Joey asked.

"I don't know what they're planning, but we need to practice for this tournament," Tony said.

Chapter Twenty-Three
THE LADDER

Pete's phone buzzed during practice. He glanced at the screen and saw his father's name. "Yeah, Dad?"

"Get home. Now."

"I'm at Joey's. We're practicing for —"

"I don't care what you're doing. Get home."

The line went dead and Pete set down his controller.

Joey looked up from the sofa. "What's wrong?"

"My dad. He wants me home."

"Right now?"

Pete nodded, then grabbed his backpack and headed for the door. "I'll be back later."

"Your dad gonna let you come back?" Tony asked.

"Probably not, but I'll be here."

Pete's house sat at the end of a quiet street, a two-story colonial with white siding and black shutters. His father's truck was parked in the driveway.

Pete stopped at the garage and looked at his bedroom window on the second floor. The window faced the side yard, hidden from the street by a row of hedges. The aluminum extension ladder lay in the grass next to the garage.

Pete glanced around to make sure no one was watching, then he grabbed the ladder and extended it to twenty-four feet. He carried it to the side of the house and positioned it against the wall just below his window. He tested it with his weight, pushing down on the bottom rung. Solid.

From the street, the hedges blocked the view; besides, his father never went to that side of the house.

Pete walked to the front door and went inside.

His father sat at the kitchen table, still in his work clothes. Robert Moritz was a big man, with close-cropped gray hair and a face that rarely smiled. "Sit down."

Pete dropped his backpack by the door and sat across from him.

"You've been spending too much time on those games," his father said. "Your grades are slipping, and you're never home."

"The tournament is in three days —"

"I don't want to hear about the tournament. Go to your room and do your homework. When you're done, come down for dinner, then go to bed. No phone, no computer, no games."

"But Dad —"

"This isn't a discussion."

Pete grabbed his backpack and walked upstairs. He could almost feel his father's eyes on his back the entire way.

Pete's room was on the second floor at the end of the hall. He closed the door and walked to the window.

The ladder stood exactly where he had left it.

He opened the window and checked the latch. It slid smoothly, making almost no sound. He could climb down after dinner, practice with the team, and be back before his father checked on him.

Pete sat at his desk and pulled out his homework. He worked

quickly, skipping the parts he didn't understand, and focused on getting it done rather than getting it right.

His phone buzzed. It was a text from Joey: You coming back?

Pete typed: Dad grounded me, but I can probably sneak out later.

Joey replied: We need you. 8 o'clock?

Pete looked at the ladder outside his window, and typed: I can make it.

Dinner was tense. Pete's mother served pot roast with carrots and potatoes. She knew something was wrong, but she didn't ask.

His father ate in silence, cutting his meat into precise squares. Pete pushed food around his plate and tried to look cooperative.

"Homework done?" his father asked.

"Almost."

"Finish it tonight."

"Yes, sir."

Pete finished eating and carried his plate to the sink. "Can I be excused?"

His father nodded. "Straight to bed when you're done."

"Yes, sir."

Pete climbed the stairs and went to his room. He closed the door and waited, listening. His father's footsteps moved from the kitchen to the living room. The television turned on.

Pete changed into dark clothes: black jeans, dark blue hoodie, black sneakers. He stuffed his regular clothes under his bed and grabbed his phone.

The window slid open without a sound. Pete climbed through and found the top rung of the ladder with his foot, then descended quickly, testing each rung before putting his full weight on it.

When he reached the ground, he looked back at the house. No lights had turned on.

Pete jogged down the street toward Joey's house.

. . .

Joey's bedroom was already full when Pete arrived. Tony sat on a beanbag with his controller, and Joey and Brie occupied the sofa.

"There he is," Joey said.

"You sneaked out?" Tony asked.

"Climbed out my window."

Tony shook his head. "That's bad ass."

"It's necessary." Pete grabbed a beanbag and sat down. "Let's practice."

They loaded Piney Woods and ran through the scenario three times. Pete played focused and sharp, making his shots, calling out positions. By the time they finished, they had completed two perfect runs.

"That's what I'm talking about," Joey said.

Pete checked his phone. Nine-forty-five. His father would go to bed in fifteen minutes.

"I gotta go."

"Same time tomorrow?" Joey asked.

Pete nodded. "Same time."

The street was dark when Pete jogged back to his house. Most of the neighborhood was settling in for the night.

Pete moved quietly to the side of the house. The ladder stood exactly where he had left it. He climbed quickly, his feet finding the rungs automatically in the dark.

When he reached his window, he pushed it open and climbed through. He landed softly on his bedroom floor and turned to look back at the ladder.

It was too visible. If his father looked out a window in the morning, he would see it.

Pete reached outside, and pushed the ladder sideways. The ladder tilted, then fell.

He closed the window and locked it, changed quickly into his pajamas, and shoved his dark clothes under the bed. His homework lay scattered on his desk. He gathered it up and put it in his backpack.

Footsteps sounded in the hallway. Pete dove into bed and pulled the covers up just as his door opened.

His father stood silhouetted in the doorway.

"You asleep?"

Pete kept his breathing steady and didn't answer.

His father stood there for a moment, then closed the door.

Pete waited until he heard his father's bedroom door close, then he let out a long breath.

Chapter Twenty-Four
RITCHIE RETURNS

Rain hammered against the windows of Joey's house. Inside, the team practiced with Brie for the third night in a row.

Ritchie stood on the porch, his hands in his pockets. Rain ran down his face and dripped off his nose. When no one answered, he buttoned his coat tightly, ran to the bedroom window, and knocked.

Joey heard the knock on the window. "Who the hell is that?"

Pete parted the blinds and looked outside. "It's Ritchie. I'll let him in."

Pete answered the door to see Ritchie standing outside, soaked and shivering. "What's up? You need something?"

"Yeah, a dry place to stay. I'm freezing." Ritchie turned his head, showing a bruised face and a large gash that was still bleeding.

"I didn't even do nothing. Came home and my dad started wailing away with his stick." Ritchie wiped away tears. "I got nowhere to go."

Pete looked closer at the cut. "Come on in. We'll get you bandaged."

Ritchie's voice lowered to almost a whisper. "Y'all practicing?"

Pete shifted his weight from one foot to the other and lowered his head. "You told us you quit."

Ritchie waved his hand in the air. "C'mon, you know I didn't mean it."

Pete shook his head, then looked Ritchie in the eyes. "We replaced you with Brie. She's inside now."

Ritchie leaned his head forward and raised his eyebrows. "You replaced me? You didn't wait long."

"Christ, Ritchie, we're in a tournament. We couldn't play with three players."

Ritchie bit his lip and nodded. "Okay."

He turned and started to walk away.

"Get in here. You can't stay out in the rain, and you can't go home. Besides, you've got to get your face bandaged."

Ritchie stood in the rain, then shrugged. "All right."

Pete called Joey, who got bandages from the cabinet and handed them to Ritchie. "Come to the bedroom when you finish."

Ritchie stared and looked as if he was tearing up. "They won't mind?"

Joey walked over and hugged Ritchie. "No one's going to mind. In fact, if you want to be the fifth team member, you're in. You and Brie can probably take turns playing. If you do that, you'll get the same share of the winnings, if we win."

Ritchie's face lit up. "Really? You'd do that?"

Joey rubbed his eyes. "Don't be an ass. We already voted on it."

Joey headed toward the bedroom.

"Be right there," Ritchie said.

Chapter Twenty-Five
SYRIAN SURPRISE

Syria

Cyrus sipped tea at the table and scowled while waiting for the others to show. The safe house in Damascus was sparse, furnished with only the essentials: a table, four chairs, and a comm unit mounted on the wall. The windows were shuttered, blocking the afternoon sun.

As the team members arrived, they took their seats, eyeing Cyrus warily once they noticed his attitude. First came Rizwan, his movements precise and economical as he pulled out a chair across from Cyrus.

Then Sandof entered, glancing between Cyrus and the empty seat before sitting down quietly.

Cyrus glared at Shaklam as he followed the others into the house. The youngest member of the team looked exhausted, his left leg bandaged beneath his tactical vest. "Why am I not surprised that you're the last to arrive?"

"I was detained," Shaklam said.

"Like you were in the Piney Woods?"

Shaklam's jaw tightened, but he said nothing. He moved toward the empty chair beside Sandof.

Cyrus took another sip of his tea, letting the silence stretch. Rizwan and Sandof shifted in their seats, waiting.

When Cyrus set the cup down, the ceramic made a sharp click against the wooden table. "And why did you go to the teleport location when you were injured?"

"Because I was —"

"If you were injured, that means the enemy was nearby. All the more reason to keep your distance."

Shaklam opened his mouth to respond, then closed it. His face flushed red.

Rizwan cleared his throat. "Perhaps we should —"

Cyrus held up one hand, silencing him. His eyes never left Shaklam. "You compromised the extraction point. You know the protocols. Injured operatives proceed to secondary locations. The primary teleport site is reserved for mission-critical personnel and equipment."

"I was mission-critical," Shaklam said, his voice quiet but firm. "I had the data core."

"The data core you were supposed to upload remotely before extraction." Cyrus leaned forward. "The data core you held onto because you wanted to personally deliver it. Because you wanted credit for the retrieval."

"That's not true," Shaklam said.

Sandof spoke up. "Cyrus, he got the core out. Whatever his reasons for doing what he did, the mission objective was achieved."

"At what cost?" Cyrus asked. He turned his attention to Sandof. "How many enemy combatants were within visual range of the extraction point when Shaklam arrived?"

Sandof hesitated. "Unknown."

"Since you refuse to answer, I will. There were four confirmed hostiles within fifty meters of our primary teleport location." Cyrus looked around the table.

"A location we've used for three previous operations. A location that is now burned because one team member didn't follow basic protocol."

Shaklam's hands curled into fists on the table. "I made a judgment call in the field. I was being pursued. I had to —"

"You had to follow orders," Cyrus said, his voice sharp. "That's all you had to do."

Rizwan leaned back in his chair, his dark eyes studying both Cyrus and Shaklam. The second oldest member of the team had seen this kind of confrontation before. He remained silent, waiting to see how it played out.

Cyrus shook his head. "If you weren't already trained for the mission, I'd eliminate you myself."

The room went silent. No one moved. The threat hung in the air, and everyone knew Cyrus meant it. He had terminated operatives before — and for less.

Shaklam folded his hands and bowed his head. "My apologies to all."

"Your apologies mean nothing if the enemy intercepted that transmission," Cyrus said.

He turned to Rizwan. "What's the latest intelligence from the Piney Woods sector?"

Rizwan pulled a tablet from his vest and activated it. "Enemy communications increased significantly two hours ago. They're mobilizing a search team. Four operatives, fully equipped for extended operations in forested terrain."

"They're looking for the teleport site," Sandof said.

"Correct," Rizwan said. "And based on their communication patterns, it's only a matter of time before they pinpoint the exact location."

Cyrus turned back to Shaklam. "When you reached the teleport location, you used the comm. Is that correct?"

"Yes," Shaklam said.

"Did the enemy hear you when you called on the com?"

Shaklam's eyes dropped to the table. "I don't think so ... but it's possible."

Sandof cursed under his breath. Rizwan set down his tablet with more force than necessary.

"I used burst transmission," Shaklam said quickly. "Standard encryption. It would take them weeks to —"

"They have quantum processors," Cyrus interrupted. "It would take them minutes, not weeks. And you know this because it was in the pre-mission briefing. The briefing you apparently didn't pay attention to."

Shaklam said nothing. His face had gone pale.

Rizwan spoke, his voice measured and calm. "What's the damage assessment? How much time do we have?"

"We have approximately eighteen hours before they locate the exact coordinates of the teleport site," Cyrus said. "Once they have that, they'll set up an ambush. Anyone using that location after that will walk into a kill zone. Or a potential kill zone."

"So we're compromised," Rizwan said.

"Unless we neutralize the GhostWalkers." Cyrus looked directly at Shaklam. "You will be the one to take care of them."

Shaklam scrunched his eyebrows. He appeared confused. "Take care of them?"

"Yes, take care of them," Cyrus said. "You created this problem. You will solve it."

"You want me to eliminate the whole team?"

"I want you to neutralize the threat to our extraction site," Cyrus said. "How you accomplish that is up to you. But it needs to be done before our first extraction. That gives you sixteen hours."

Shaklam swallowed hard. "Alone?"

"You created this mess alone," Cyrus said. "This is non-negotiable."

Shaklam stood slowly. The bandage on his leg showing spots of fresh blood. "I'll take care of it."

Sandof squeezed Shaklam's shoulder as they left. "Good luck, brother."

Then they were gone, and Shaklam was alone with Cyrus.

Cyrus poured himself another cup of tea. He didn't offer one to Shaklam. "Sit down," Cyrus said.

Shaklam sat.

Cyrus studied him for a long moment, sipping his tea. When he finally spoke, his voice was calmer but no less serious. "Do you understand why I'm angry with you?"

"Because I violated protocol," Shaklam said.

"No," Cyrus said. "I'm angry because you put your ego ahead of the mission. You wanted to be the hero who delivered the data core personally. You wanted the recognition."

"That's not —"

"Don't lie to me," Cyrus said. "I've been doing this for twenty years."

Shaklam's jaw tightened, but he said nothing.

Cyrus set down his teacup. "The GhostWalkers have four men. They are no less elite trackers and soldiers than we are. They're well-armed and they know the terrain. Your job is to stop them before they reach the teleport site and learn how to operate it."

"How?" Shaklam asked.

"I don't care how you do it, as long as our extraction point remains secure."

"What about my leg?"

"What about it?"

"I was injured in the Piney Woods. The wound hasn't fully healed."

"Then you'll work through the pain," Cyrus said. "Or you'll fail. Either way, it's your problem, not mine."

He stood, signaling the meeting was over. Shaklam stood as well.

Shaklam left the room, his footsteps echoing in the hallway.

He heard footsteps in the hallway. Rizwan appeared in the doorway.

"Is he ready?" Rizwan asked.

"He will be," Cyrus said. "Or he won't. Either way, we'll know soon enough."

Rizwan entered and sat down across from Cyrus. "You're hard on him."

"He needs to be pushed," Cyrus said. "Let's see what happens in Houston."

Chapter Twenty-Six
A REVELATION

Joey addressed the other team members. "Now we know how they got behind us without being seen. They're using the teleport stations, just like we did when we ended up in my front yard."

"How does that help?" Brie asked.

"At the beginning of the next game, we'll send you and Pete to the ammo shack. Tony and I will stay near the entrance. If you see them go into the shack, let us know. We'll know they're about to teleport, and we can position ourselves accordingly. If they come out of the shack normally, take them out."

Pete frowned. "Suppose they go somewhere else?"

"We don't care if they go somewhere else. We'll hunker down and stay alert, and you two can stay still until they come out, then take them."

Joey stared at each of them. "Now let's get practicing. We're already down one game."

"Should we tell your dad about this?" Pete asked.

Joey shook his head. "Not yet."

Tony stepped forward. "Why not? He might have some insight into how the teleport system works. At least, I assume the FBI would know about something like this."

"We already know how it works," Joey said. "We figured that out when we teleported to the front yard. The difference is, WolfDen has been using it in competition. They know the strategy. We don't. Not yet."

"But that's a big head start they've got," Pete said. "It gives them a damn big advantage."

"Exactly," Joey said. "They've been practicing with it and learning the best places to teleport to. That's how they've won five tournaments in a row."

Pete nodded slowly. "Now that we know what they're doing, we just need to practice using it ourselves."

Joey's jaw tightened. "Right. And we need to figure out how to counter it when they use it against us."

Brie spoke up. "The teleport feature was briefly mentioned by DeathMaster, but they didn't give us much detail. We had to experiment to figure it out. WolfDen must have done the same thing, just earlier than we did."

Joey nodded. "I wish I'd paid more attention to those hints in the instructions. We could have been practicing with it this whole time."

Tony chimed in. "Not everything is in the instructions, Joey. They leave some things for players to figure out on their own. This is definitely one of those things, but don't worry. We'll catch up. Let's just focus on the plan."

Tony was already working through scenarios they might face and contingency plans they could use. WolfDen had beaten them in the first game because they'd mastered the teleport mechanics. Now that the GhostWalkers understood what was happening, the playing field was level.

Joey pulled out his phone and opened the tournament app, scrolling through the stats from the first game. WolfDen's movement patterns made perfect sense now. They were using the teleport stations to reposition quickly, hitting the GhostWalkers from unexpected angles. Not anymore they won't.

"All right, let's get going. Everybody knows the plan."

. . .

The team deployed to their assigned stations. The ammo shack sat in the center of the map, accessible from all sides. It was the one place where players could resupply without having to return to their spawn point. But it was also a vulnerable position, exposed to fire from multiple angles.

Joey positioned himself near the eastern entrance while Tony climbed to his usual sniper perch. Brie and Pete made their way to the ammo shack, moving carefully through the forest terrain.

"GH5 in position," Brie said through the comm.

"GH3 in position," Pete added.

Joey scanned the area. "Tony, you got eyes on the shack?"

"Affirmative. Clear sight line to all entrances."

"Good. Brie, Pete, I want you to test the teleport station. See if you can figure out where else it connects to."

Brie entered the ammo shack and approached the monitor. The coordinates displayed were different from what they'd seen before. She studied the keypad on the wall.

"There's no manual entry option here," she said. "Just three preset buttons. Red, blue, and green."

"Try the red one," Joey said.

Brie pressed it. The coordinates changed on screen: 44° 52' 18.36" N: -93° 21' 42.88" W

"Nothing happened," Pete said. "Maybe you have to enter the booth?"

Brie moved to the phone booth structure and stepped inside. She pressed the red button again. The familiar whirring sound started, and suddenly she was gone.

"Brie?" Joey's voice came through the comm. "Where are you?"

Static.

"Brie, do you copy?"

More static, then her voice broke through. "I'm in a different structure. Looks like another ammo shack, but in a different location. I'm seeing coordinates for this spot."

"Can you get back?"

"There's a return button. Green. I'm pressing it now."

The whirring sound repeated, and Brie reappeared in the original shack.

Pete grinned. "That's how they've been doing it. They teleport to different supply points across the map."

"How many stations are there?" Joey asked.

Brie checked the monitor again. "Three preset locations from here. Red, blue, green. Each one probably connects to different spots."

Tony's voice came through. "That means WolfDen has been bouncing around the map, hitting us from angles we couldn't predict."

"Not anymore," Joey said. "Brie, Pete, mark all three locations. We need to know where each button takes you."

Over the next hour, the team mapped out the teleport network. There were five ammo shacks across the map, each with three preset destinations. The system created a web of quick-travel points that could turn a slow tactical game into rapid chaos.

Joey pulled everyone together after the mapping session. "All right, here's what we know. WolfDen's been using these stations to outflank us. They can teleport behind our positions faster than we can react."

"So how do we counter it?" Pete asked.

"We use it better than they do," Brie said. "They expect us to play traditionally. We hit them with their own strategy."

Tony nodded. "If we control the stations, we control the map."

Joey pointed to the diagram he'd drawn. "Station Alpha is here, near the northern entrance. Bravo is center-west. Charlie is center-east. Delta is south. Echo is at the extraction point."

"WolfDen's going to rush for Station Alpha," Tony said. "They always take the high ground first."

"Let them," Joey said. "We'll take Bravo and Charlie. That gives us control of the center. When they try to teleport behind us, we'll already be in position."

Brie studied the map. "What about Delta?"

"Too exposed. Whoever holds Delta is a sitting duck for snipers."

"Unless," Brie said slowly, "we use Delta as bait."

Joey looked at her. "Go on."

"WolfDen knows we're inexperienced with the teleports. They'll assume we don't understand the system yet. What if we let them see one of us at Delta, make it look like we're trying to figure it out?"

"They'll teleport in to take us out," Pete said.

"Exactly. But we'll be waiting for them."

Tony grinned. "That's brutal."

"That's winning," Brie said.

Joey considered it. "All right. New plan. Brie, you're the bait at Delta. Pete, you're with her, hidden. Tony stays at Alpha for overwatch. I'll hold Bravo."

"What about Charlie?" Pete asked.

"Charlie's our fallback. If things go wrong, we regroup there and reset."

The team nodded. Tony checked his watch. "We've got forty-five minutes before the next game."

"Then let's run it," Joey said. "Brie, you good with being exposed?"

She smiled. "I'm black, Joey. I know how to handle being a target."

Pete winced, but Joey just nodded. "Fair point. Let's move."

They ran through the strategy three times. Each iteration got smoother, faster. Brie played her part perfectly, acting confused at Station Delta while Pete hid in the nearby brush. When the practice opponents teleported in, Pete took them out before they could react.

On the third run, Tony spotted a flaw. "Brie, when you're at Delta, you're checking the monitor too long. Real players will notice you're not actually confused."

"What should I do?"

"Press buttons. Look frustrated. Make it seem like you're trying different combinations."

Brie tried it again. This time, her performance was convincing.

Joey watched from his position at Bravo. The pieces were coming together. WolfDen had the experience, but the GhostWalkers had figured out their secret. And now they had a plan.

Pete rejoined the group after the final practice run. "You really think this will work?"

"It has to," Joey said. "Now that we know how to use the teleport stations, we're on equal footing with WolfDen. We just need to execute better than they do."

Tony cleaned his rifle scope. "What if they change their strategy?"

"Then we adapt," Joey said. "But I'm guessing they're confident. They won one game using their teleport advantage. They'll probably stick with what works."

Brie sat on the couch, studying the map on her phone. "There's something else we should consider."

"What's that?" Joey asked.

"If we know about the teleports now, and we're planning around them, maybe other teams have figured it out too."

Pete shook his head. "I talked to some guys from other teams. WolfDen demolished every one of them."

"Yeah," Joey said. "But none of them had Brie sneaking around and watching WolfDen teleport out of a shack."

Brie looked up. "So we have an advantage they don't know we have."

"Exactly."

Tony checked his equipment. "Should we tell the other teams?"

Joey shook his head. "They can figure it out on their own, just like we did. Right now, we need to focus on beating WolfDen."

He looked at his watch. "We've got thirty minutes before the next game. Let's run it one more time, and make sure everyone knows their position. And let's practice a few teleport sequences. I want everyone comfortable with the timing."

The team nodded and moved back to their starting positions.

Twenty minutes later, they gathered in Joey's room. The energy was different now. Focused. Determined.

Joey's phone buzzed. A message from the tournament organizers: *Game 2 begins in 10 minutes. Map: Piney Woods. Report to stations.*

"That's us," Tony said.

Brie stood and stretched. "Piney Woods. That's good for us. More cover, harder for them to spot our movements."

"Unless they teleport right on top of us," Pete said.

"They won't," Joey said. "We control the center. They have to come through us to get to the stations."

Tony pulled on his headset. "Everyone clear on the plan?"

Three nods.

"Then let's go win this thing."

They logged into the game, and the familiar interface loaded. The tournament bracket showed their position: GhostWalkers vs WolfDen, Game 2 of 3. Winner moves to semifinals.

The map materialized around them. Piney Woods at night, just like their practice session. But this time, it counted.

Joey took a deep breath. "All right, GhostWalkers. Execute the plan. Stay sharp. And remember, they don't know we know."

"Let's hunt some wolves," Brie said.

The countdown began.

Five.

Four.

Three.

Two.

One.

The game started.

Chapter Twenty-Seven
SENATOR RICHARDSON

Sean poured a cup of coffee and was on his way to the office when Director Samuels called him in.

"What is it, boss?"

"You get anything on that chatter we heard about last week?"

Sean shook his head. "I talked to the CIA. The said they've had five people on it, but there's been nothing new so far. Not even a hint."

"Keep your eyes open. It sounded credible to me."

"You want me to ask them to put more men on it?"

"No, I'm already catching shit about spending, and if they go with more men, they'll sure as hell bill us for it. Go with what we've got."

Sean took a sip of his coffee and set the cup on the edge of Samuels' desk. "We should be good. All suspected targets are protected: the president and vice president, the speaker, and the senators and congressmen who are known opponents of the Middle Eastern terrorists. The only possible vulnerability — in the near term — is Senator Richardson. She's giving a speech tomorrow, but she's well-guarded."

Director Samuels tapped his pen on the desk, then looked up at Sean. "Add a few more men to her detail, just to make sure."

"Maybe she should call off her speech?"

Samuels shook his head. "She's up for reelection, so fat chance of that."

Sean picked up his coffee and moved toward the door, then stopped. "The language in those intercepts was specific. They mentioned a high-value target at a public event. Richardson fits that profile."

"So do a dozen other politicians giving speeches this week," Samuels said.

"True, but she's the only one who's been vocal about increasing drone strikes in Yemen. That makes her a priority target."

Samuels set down his pen. "What's your gut telling you?"

Sean hesitated. His gut had been wrong before, but it had also saved lives. "My gut says this is real. The chatter has been too detailed to be just noise. Someone's planning something."

"But we don't know what or where."

"No, sir. That's the problem."

Samuels leaned back in his chair and studied Sean for a long moment. "How many agents do you have working this?"

"We've got two at each of the potential target's speeches, and four at Richardson's. Martinez is running point, and Chen is handling backup. Brooks and Kelly are coordinating with Secret Service. And Thompson's working the CIA, still trying to identify who's doing the talking."

"Any progress on identification?"

"Not yet. The intercepts are coming through encrypted channels, bouncing between servers in three different countries. They're trying to trace the origin, but it's slow going."

"How slow?"

"They said it be could be weeks."

Samuels cursed under his breath. "We don't have weeks. If something's happening tomorrow, we need answers today."

Samuels picked up his pen again and pointed it at Sean. "I want hourly updates. If anything changes, I want to know about it immediately."

"Understood."

Sean turned to leave, but Samuels called him back.

"One more thing. If you get solid intelligence that Richardson is the target, come to me first — not Secret Service, and not her campaign staff. We'll make the call together on whether to shut it down."

"Yes, sir."

Sean left the office and headed down the hallway toward the operations center. His coffee had gone cold, but he drank it anyway. He'd need the caffeine before this day was over.

Martinez looked up as he entered. "Samuels give you the green light for extra resources?"

"No. We work with what we've got."

"That figures." Martinez pulled up a new screen on her monitor. "We did pick up something interesting about twenty minutes ago. Another intercept, same encryption pattern as the others."

Sean moved behind her desk and looked at the screen. "What does it say?"

"Still decrypting, but we pulled out a few key words. Delivery confirmed."

Sean felt his stomach tighten. "Where did it originate?"

"We're still tracing it, but preliminary analysis suggests it came from somewhere in the Houston metro area."

"Houston. Where Richardson's giving her speech."

"Could be a coincidence," Martinez said.

"Or it could be confirmation." Sean pulled out his phone. "I need to talk to Secret Service. Get me the agent in charge of Richardson's detail."

Martinez made the call and handed him the phone.

"This is Special Agent Carver," a voice said on the other end.

"Agent Carver, this is Sean Lugullo with the FBI. I need to brief you on a potential threat to Senator Richardson at her speech tomorrow."

"We've already been briefed. Your office sent over a threat assessment this morning."

"That assessment just changed. We've intercepted new communications that suggest the threat is imminent and specific to tomorrow's speech."

There was a pause. "How credible is this intelligence?"

"Credible enough that Director Samuels wants additional agents on Richardson's detail."

"We've already increased coverage to a dozen agents and the venue's been swept twice. We're as ready as we're going to be."

"I'd like to do another sweep," Sean said. "With a specialized team."

"What kind of specialized team?"

"Chemical and biological threat assessment."

Another pause. "You think this is a chemical attack?"

"I think we need to rule it out," Sean said. "The language in the intercepts is unusual. They talk about packages and deliveries. That doesn't sound like a conventional assassination attempt."

"All right," Carver said. "Coordinate with my team. We'll give you access to the venue at sixteen hundred hours today. But make it quick. We've got a final security briefing at eighteen hundred."

"Understood. Thank you, Agent Carver."

Sean hung up and handed the phone back to Martinez. "Get the HAZMAT team mobilized. I want them at the convention center by sixteen hundred."

"On it," Martinez said.

Sean walked to the operations board and stared at the timeline they'd built. Seven intercepts over the past ten days, all using similar language, all suggesting a coordinated attack on a high-value target. And now, less than twenty-four hours before Richardson's speech, they had confirmation that something was happening in Houston.

Chen approached from the other side of the room. "I finished the linguistic analysis on the intercepts. The syntax patterns suggest the speakers are native Arabic speakers, probably from the Gulf region. Saudi or Emirati, most likely, but don't bank on that. It could be Syrian too."

"That narrows it down," Sean said. "What about the encryption?"

"Military grade. Not something you pick up off the shelf. Whoever's behind this has access to sophisticated technology."

"And training," Sean added.

"Yeah. These aren't amateurs."

Sean checked his watch. It was just past eleven in the morning.

Richardson's speech was scheduled for two in the afternoon tomorrow. That gave them roughly twenty-seven hours to identify the threat, locate the attackers, and neutralize them before they could act.

Twenty-seven hours to prevent whatever was coming.

He turned to his team. "All right, listen up. We're going to assume the threat is real and the target is Richardson. That means we have one day to figure out what they're planning and how they're planning to do it."

Martinez, I want you and Brooks at the convention center for the sweep. Chen, keep working the intercepts. See if you can pull anything else out of that encryption. Thompson, I need you to shake down every source we have in the Middle Eastern community. Someone knows something. Find them."

He paused and looked around the room. "And people, be smart about this. If this is what we think it is, these guys are professionals. They're not going to make it easy for us."

The team dispersed to their stations. Sean returned to his office and closed the door. He sat at his desk and pulled up Richardson's schedule for tomorrow. She was speaking at the Greater Houston Business Coalition luncheon. Fifteen hundred attendees, mostly local business leaders and political donors. The kind of crowd that would generate maximum media coverage.

The kind of crowd that will maximize casualties if something goes wrong.

He opened his desk drawer and pulled out a bottle of antacids, popped two tablets and chased them with the remainder of his cold coffee.

Tomorrow will be a very long day.

Chapter Twenty-Eight
PREPARING FOR A SPEECH

The Next Day

Senator Richardson's office exuded power. Dark wood paneling covered the walls, and a massive mahogany desk dominated the center of the room. Legal briefs were stacked neatly on one corner, and framed accolades lined the wall behind the desk. A portrait of her granddaughter hung prominently on the main wall, the only personal touch in an otherwise austere space.

Richardson stood before a full-length mirror near the window, evaluating her reflection. She adjusted her hair, then smoothed the front of her navy blue suit jacket. Three makeup artists hovered around her like bees, brushes and compacts in hand.

She shooed them away with a flick of her wrist. "I've dressed myself for forty years. I don't need help now."

The makeup artists exchanged glances but backed off. One of them gathered her supplies and moved to the corner of the room, waiting to see if she'd be needed.

Richardson's aide, Margaret Choi, stood nearby holding a luxurious wool coat. She was in her forties, assertive but cautious, and she'd learned over the years when to push and when to stay silent. This looked like a time to push.

"Senator, about today's speech," Margaret said.

Richardson continued examining her reflection. "What about it?"

"I reviewed the draft you sent over this morning. There are a few sections that concern me."

"Such as?"

Margaret set the coat on a nearby chair and pulled out her tablet. "The section about increased military action in Yemen. And the part where you call for zero tolerance on refugee admissions."

"Both perfectly reasonable positions," Richardson said. She turned from the mirror and faced her aide. "What's the problem?"

"The problem is how you phrase them. You need to be careful not to say anything that could be interpreted as inflammatory."

"Inflammatory to whom?"

Margaret hesitated, then spoke carefully. "Remember, don't say anything to anger the Blacks, Asians, Latinos, or the LGBT community."

Richardson cast a sideways glance at her aide. Her irritation was obvious. "I don't care who I offend. Those terrorists need to be dealt with."

"Senator, please —"

"It's your job to fix what I say *after* I say it. That's why I pay you. I say what needs to be said, and you smooth it over for the press."

Margaret closed her tablet. "That's becoming increasingly difficult to do. Social media doesn't give us time to smooth things over anymore. When you say something controversial, it's everywhere within minutes."

"Good," Richardson said. "Let people hear the truth for once."

"The truth won't help you if you lose your reelection."

Richardson moved to her desk and picked up the speech she'd be delivering in less than two hours. She scanned the pages, her lips moving slightly as she read certain passages.

"This speech is fine," she said. "It says exactly what needs to be said. The American people are tired of coddling terrorists. They're tired of watching their tax dollars go to people who want to destroy us.

They want leadership. They want someone who isn't afraid to call evil what it is."

"They also want someone who can win elections," Margaret said. "And inflammatory rhetoric — even if it's true — can cost you votes."

Richardson set down the speech and looked at her aide. "How many points am I up in the polls?"

"Twelve points as of yesterday."

"Twelve points. Against an opponent who's been campaigning for eight months. Do you know why I'm up twelve points?"

"Because you speak your mind," Margaret said.

"Exactly. Because I don't pander. Because I don't check every word against some focus group to make sure it won't hurt anyone's feelings." Richardson walked to the window and looked out at the Houston skyline. "People are scared, Margaret. They're scared of terrorism, scared of losing their jobs, scared their children won't have the same opportunities they had. And when people are scared, they want leaders who project strength. Not politicians who apologize for everything."

Margaret joined her at the window. "I understand that, Senator. And I'm not asking you to change your message. I'm just asking you to be strategic about how you deliver it."

"Strategic," Richardson repeated. She turned away from the window. "You want me to water it down."

"I want you to be effective. There's a difference between being bold and being reckless."

Richardson walked back to the mirror and examined her reflection one more time. She adjusted her collar, then nodded to herself.

"The speech stands as written," she said. "No changes."

Margaret sighed. "At least let me review it one more time before you go on stage. Maybe we can soften some of the language without changing the substance."

"You have fifteen minutes," Richardson said. "I need to leave for the venue by noon."

One of the makeup artists approached cautiously. "Senator, if I could just touch up your lipstick —"

"Fine," Richardson said. "But make it quick."

While the makeup artist worked, Margaret pulled up the speech on her tablet and began reading through it again. She made notes in the margins, highlighting phrases that would likely generate controversy.

Richardson watched her in the mirror. "How bad is it?"

"The section on drone strikes will get headlines," Margaret said. "So will the part about closing the border to all refugees from Muslim-majority countries."

"Both necessary policies."

"Perhaps. But the way you phrase them —" Margaret paused, searching for the right words. "You compare refugees to an invading army. That's going to generate backlash."

"Let it generate backlash," Richardson said. "I'd rather be attacked for telling the truth than praised for lying."

The makeup artist finished and stepped back. Richardson examined the result, nodded approval, and dismissed her with a wave.

Margaret set down her tablet. "Senator, I've been with you for six years. I've helped you navigate some difficult situations. But this speech worries me. Not because of the substance, but because of the timing."

Richardson turned to face her. "What about the timing?"

"You're giving this speech three weeks before the election. If you generate controversy now, we won't have time to recover before people go to the polls."

"We're up twelve points," Richardson said. "We don't need to recover from anything."

"Twelve points can evaporate in a news cycle," Margaret said. "One viral video, one poorly worded statement taken out of context, and suddenly we're in a close race."

Richardson picked up her coat from the chair and slipped it on. She checked her appearance one final time in the mirror, then turned to her aide.

"I appreciate your concern, Margaret. I do. But I didn't get into politics to play it safe. I got into it to make a difference. And sometimes making a difference means taking risks."

She walked to the door, then paused and looked back. "Are you coming?"

Margaret grabbed her bag and tablet. "Of course."

"Good. And stop worrying so much. Everything's going to be fine."

They left the office and walked down the hallway toward the elevator. Two Secret Service agents fell into step behind them, their eyes constantly scanning for threats.

In the elevator, Margaret tried one more time. "Senator, what if we just delay the speech? Give me a week to work with you on the language, find ways to say the same things with less controversy."

Richardson shook her head. "The speech is today. It's been scheduled for months. Fifteen hundred people are expecting to hear from me. I'm not going to disappoint them."

The elevator doors opened on the ground floor, and they walked out to a black SUV that waited at the curb, engine running. The Secret Service agents moved ahead, checking the vehicle and surrounding area before signaling that it was clear.

Richardson climbed into the back seat. Margaret slid in beside her.

As the SUV pulled away from the curb, Richardson pulled out her phone and scrolled through messages. Most were from supporters, wishing her luck with the speech. A few were from fellow senators, offering advice on how to handle the media afterward.

She ignored them all and opened the speech file on her phone. She read through it one more time, making small mental notes about emphasis and pacing. The words were strong, direct, uncompromising. Exactly what the moment required.

Margaret sat quietly beside her, still reviewing her own notes. After several minutes of silence, she spoke.

"Senator, I need to ask you something."

Richardson looked up from her phone. "What?"

"Why is this speech so important to you? I've seen you give hundreds of speeches. But this one — you seem particularly invested in it."

Richardson was quiet for a moment, then gestured toward the framed photo she always kept in her briefcase. It showed her granddaughter, Emma, at her fifth birthday party.

"Emma asked me a question last week," Richardson said. "She asked if the world was safe. If bad people could hurt her."

Margaret waited.

"I told her the truth," Richardson continued. "I told her there are bad people in the world. People who want to hurt us. But I also told her that good people are fighting to keep her safe. And that as long as good people refuse to give up, refuse to back down, she'll be okay."

She tucked the phone back in her pocket. "This speech is about keeping that promise. About showing Emma — and every other child in this country — that we're still willing to fight. That we haven't given up."

Margaret nodded slowly. "I understand, Senator. I do. I just hope the message comes across the way you intend it."

"It will," Richardson said. "Have faith."

The SUV merged onto the highway, heading toward the convention center. Traffic was light, and they'd arrive with time to spare. Richardson closed her eyes and took a deep breath, centering herself for what lay ahead.

In ninety minutes, she'd stand before fifteen hundred people and deliver the most important speech of her campaign. The words would generate controversy, spark debates, and probably cost her some support among moderates.

But they'd also energize her base, demonstrate her courage, and remind voters why they'd supported her in the first place.

She opened her eyes and looked out the window at the Houston skyline. Somewhere out there, people were preparing to listen to what she had to say. Some would agree, some would disagree, and some would hate her for it.

That was politics. That was the price of leadership.

And Senator Elizabeth Richardson had never been afraid of paying that price.

Chapter Twenty-Nine
KEEP YOUR EYES ON THE SHACK

Joey settled into his seat on the sofa, drew heavily on his vape, and blew a cloud of smoke in Tony's direction.

Tony turned and stared, his eyes narrowed.

"Yeah, yeah. I'm vaping, Tony. Live with it. And once you've gotten used to that, get ready. This is a critical game.

"Don't worry. Quit vaping, and we'll win," Tony said.

Brie and Pete high-fived Tony. "That's the spirit, T," Brie said.

"Damn right, we will," Pete said.

Once they entered their DNA, Brie and Pete headed toward the shack and took positions west of it. Joey and Tony stayed back and hunkered behind a few large rocks surrounded by trees. They waited for WolfDen to approach from the rear.

Shaklam crept up to the shack from the north and went inside. Brie and Pete waited to see if any of the other WolfDen team showed, but no one did. And after a few minutes, Shaklam didn't emerge.

"Joey, this is Brie. We've got one of them inside the shack, but he's been out of sight for almost five minutes. There's been no sign of the others."

Pete tapped her arm to draw attention. "I think I heard noise coming from the shack."

Brie whispered into the mic. "Signing off, Joey. Pete heard something that we're going to check out, but we'll keep you posted."

"Stay put, Brie. We're in position to handle any advance."

Brie signaled Pete to stay low and quiet.

Joey tugged Tony's sleeve and pointed south. Two of the WolfDen team advanced from the rear and quickly moved toward Pete.

Tony tilted his head and listened. He nodded as leaves rustled, then signaled Joey and whispered into the mic. "Sighting confirmed. Two approaching from the south."

Joey looked through his binoculars until he saw them. "I got a bead on them, Tony. Should we let 'em get closer?"

Tony looked through the scope on his rifle. "I've got a bead on them too. Wait for me to fire."

When they got within fifty yards, Tony opened fire and hit one in the head. The noise of the rifle, even suppressed, was deafening in the silence. He quickly sighted in another and hit him with a chest shot, then a leg shot, taking him out.

Joey noticed a third member peek around the corner of a building and waited for him to advance. As soon as he got close enough, Joey opened fire, taking him out. Ecstatic, he called Brie. "Three down. We're coming your way."

"Don't get cocky. I've seen one person take out a whole team," Brie said.

Joey moved carefully through the trees, keeping low. Tony followed twenty yards behind, covering their rear. They moved in silence, communicating only through hand signals.

As they approached the shack, Brie's voice came through again. "Joey, stop. Don't come any closer."

"What's going on?"

"The shack is empty. Shaklam's gone. The teleport booth is active."

Joey stopped behind a thick pine tree. "He used it?"

"Had to. There's no other way out."

"Where did he go?"

"That's what we're trying to figure out. The monitor shows three possible destinations from here."

Tony caught up to Joey and crouched beside him. "If he teleported, he could be anywhere on the map by now."

"Or right behind us," Pete said.

Joey scanned the area. "Brie, Pete, get out of there. Move to the extraction point. We'll meet you there."

"Negative," Brie said. "If we leave, they could use this station to hit us from behind."

"Then one of you stays, one moves."

"I'll stay," Brie said. "Pete, head to extraction."

Pete hesitated. "You sure?"

"Go."

Joey watched Pete emerge from cover and sprint east toward the extraction point. He made it twenty yards before a shot rang out.

Pete dove behind a fallen log. "Contact. One shooter, southeast."

Tony swung his rifle around, searching for the target. "I don't see him."

"He's in the trees," Pete said. "I can't get a clean shot."

Joey keyed his mic. "Brie, can you see Pete's position from the shack?"

"Negative. Too much foliage."

"Then we've got a problem."

Another shot hit the log near Pete's head. He pressed himself flat against the ground.

"He's got me pinned," Pete said. "I can't move."

Tony finally spotted movement in the trees. He fired once, then twice. A body fell from a high branch and hit the ground hard.

"Target down," Tony said.

"That's four," Joey said. "One left."

Pete got to his feet and brushed dirt off his vest. "Thanks, T."

"Don't mention it."

Brie's voice cut through. "Guys, the monitor just changed. Someone accessed the network from Station Echo."

"That's the extraction point," Joey said.

"Which means Shaklam teleported there. He's waiting for us."

Joey thought fast. Station Echo was the endgame. They had to get there to win, but if Shaklam was dug in, he had the advantage.

"Brie, can you teleport to Echo from where you are?"

"Let me check." A pause. "Affirmative. The blue button goes to Echo."

"Don't use it. He'll hear you arrive."

"Then what's the plan?"

Joey looked at Tony. "We go in traditional. Slow approach, multiple angles. Make him think we don't know he's there."

"He'll pick us off one by one," Pete said.

"Not if we're smart about it." Joey pulled up the map on his display. "Pete, you approach from the east. Tony, take the high ground to the west. I'll come straight up the middle."

"What about me?" Brie asked.

"Stay at the shack. If things go wrong, you teleport to Echo and clean up."

"That's a terrible plan."

"You got a better one?"

Brie went quiet for a moment. "Actually, yeah. I do."

"I'm listening," Joey said.

"Shaklam thinks he's got the advantage at Echo. He's waiting for us to walk into his trap."

"Right."

"So we don't walk. We run."

Tony shook his head. "That's suicide."

"No, listen. He can't watch all approaches at once. If we all rush simultaneously from different angles, he has to choose a target. That gives the rest of us an opening."

Pete spoke up. "And whoever he shoots first is out."

"Better one of us than all of us," Brie said. "Besides, he's alone. Once we're in close, he's done."

Joey considered it. The plan was aggressive, risky. But it might work.

"Tony, you good with that?"

Tony sighed. "I hate it. But yeah, I'm good."

"Pete?"

"Let's do it."

"All right. Brie, you're in. Stay at the shack until we're in position, then teleport to Echo. Come in from the north. That's the one angle he won't expect."

"Copy that."

Joey checked his ammo. Full mag, one spare. He'd need to make every shot count.

"Everyone move to staging positions. We go on my mark."

The team spread out, each taking their designated route. Joey moved through the forest carefully, keeping trees between himself and the extraction point. He could see the structure now, a small elevated platform with stairs on all sides.

Shaklam would be up there somewhere, probably prone, rifle trained on the most likely approach.

Joey reached his position and keyed the mic. "GH1 in position."

"GH4 in position," Tony said.

"GH3 in position," Pete added.

They waited for Brie.

Ten seconds passed. Twenty. Thirty.

"GH5, do you copy?" Joey asked.

Static.

"Brie, do you copy?"

More static, then a faint voice. "I'm here. Had some interference. Ready when you are."

"All right. On three, we move. Fast and aggressive. Don't stop until you're at the platform."

"Copy."

"One."

Joey tightened his grip on his rifle.

"Two."

He took a deep breath.

"Three. Go, go, go."

Joey burst from cover and sprinted toward the extraction point. To his left, he saw Pete doing the same. To his right, Tony charged forward, rifle ready.

A shot rang out. Pete stumbled but kept running. Hit in the shoulder, but not a kill shot.

Another shot. This one missed Joey by inches, splintering bark from a tree beside him.

"Keep moving," Joey yelled.

He reached the stairs and started climbing. Above him, Shaklam shifted position, trying to track all three targets at once.

That's when Brie appeared.

The teleport platform materialized behind Shaklam with a soft whir. He spun around, but Brie was already firing. Two shots to the chest, one to the head.

Shaklam's character froze, then dissolved into pixels.

"Target eliminated," Brie said calmly.

The screen flashed: GHOSTWALKERS WIN.

∽

In Joey's room, the team erupted.

Pete jumped up, pumping his fist. "Yes! We did it."

Tony pulled off his headset and grinned. "That was insane."

Joey leaned back on the sofa, exhaling slowly. "That was too close."

Brie smiled. "But we won."

"Yeah. We won." Joey looked at each of them. "Good work, everyone. That's one game each. Next one decides it."

Tony stood and stretched. "When's the final game?"

Joey checked the tournament app. "Tomorrow night. Eight PM."

"Same time as before," Pete said.

"Same stakes," Brie added. "Winner goes to semifinals."

Joey nodded. "Which means we practice all day tomorrow. No excuses, no distractions."

"What map do you think it'll be?" Tony asked.

"Could be anything. We need to be ready for all of them."

Pete grabbed a water bottle from the mini fridge. "You think WolfDen will change their strategy now that we beat them?"

"Definitely," Brie said. "They know we figured out the teleports. They'll adjust."

"Then we adjust too," Joey said. "That's why we practice."

Tony sat back down. "We should review the footage from this game. See what worked and what didn't."

"Good idea." Joey pulled up the replay on his laptop. "Pete, you took a hit early. What happened?"

"I was too exposed. Should have stayed behind cover longer."

"Next time, wait for my signal before you break."

"Got it."

They spent the next hour breaking down the game, analyzing every move, every decision. Where they succeeded, where they failed, how they could improve.

By the time they finished, it was past midnight.

Brie yawned and stood up. "I should head home."

"I'll walk you out," Joey said.

They headed down the hallway. At the front door, Brie turned to him.

"We can win this, you know. The whole tournament."

"You think so?"

"I know so. WolfDen's good, but we're better. We just need to believe it."

Joey smiled. "I'm starting to."

"Good." She opened the door. "See you tomorrow. Don't be late."

"Wouldn't dream of it."

After she left, Joey returned to his room. Pete and Tony were still there, reviewing footage.

"She's right, you know," Tony said without looking up. "We can win this."

"I know," Joey said. "But first we need to figure out what WolfDen's going to throw at us next."

Pete paused the replay. "Whatever it is, we'll be ready."

Joey nodded. "Yeah. We will."

Chapter Thirty
ASSASSINATION

Shaklam entered GPS coordinates into the game system and pressed the teleport function. The world dissolved around him, and within seconds he emerged inside a van parked two blocks from the convention center where the Greater Houston Business Coalition was hosting Senator Richardson.

A game system sat on the seat next to him, the screen still glowing from the teleport sequence.

Shaklam stepped out of the van and adjusted the reporter ID hanging around his neck. The credential looked authentic because it *was* authentic.

He walked toward the convention center, joining a stream of late arrivals. Security was tight. Uniformed officers stood at every corner, and he spotted at least three plainclothes agents scanning the crowd — Secret Service, probably.

An officer making rounds through the crowd stepped in front of him. "ID, please."

Shaklam lifted the press credential and let it dangle where the officer could see it clearly. The officer studied it for a moment, then nodded toward the metal detectors. "Go through security, then check in at the press desk."

Shaklam walked through the metal detector, then collected his phone and wallet from the tray and proceeded to the press check-in.

A woman with a clipboard verified his credentials and directed him to the press section. "You're late. Most of the good spots are taken."

"That's fine," Shaklam said.

He made his way to the press area, a cordoned-off section to the left of the stage. About twenty reporters were already there, cameras ready, notepads out. He scanned the area and spotted what he was looking for: a camera bag with a red tag attached to the handle. The signal.

Shaklam positioned himself near the bag. When no one was looking, he opened it and reached inside. His fingers found the silenced pistol wrapped in a camera lens cloth. He slipped it into his jacket in one smooth motion, then closed the bag.

The weapon had been planted earlier by an operative who entered the building as part of the catering staff. The security sweep had happened hours before the weapon was positioned. By the time Secret Service did their final check, everything looked clean.

Now Shaklam had what he needed.

Richardson walked onto the stage amid a throng of applause. The crowd rose to their feet, clapping and cheering. She waved, smiled, and made her way to the podium.

She positioned herself at the center, adjusted the microphone, and took a sip of water from the glass on the podium. The crowd slowly quieted, settling back into their seats.

"Thank you," Richardson said. "Thank you all for coming today."

More applause. She waited for it to die down, then began her speech.

Shaklam watched her carefully, calculating angles and distance. She was about forty yards away. An easy shot with the weapon he carried. He'd made harder shots in training.

Richardson spoke about national security, about the threat of terrorism, about the need for strong leadership in dangerous times. The crowd ate it up, cheering after nearly every sentence.

"We cannot afford to be weak," Richardson said. "We cannot afford to hesitate. When our enemies threaten us, we must respond with overwhelming force."

The crowd erupted in applause. The noise was deafening.

Shaklam reached into his jacket and wrapped his fingers around the grip of the silenced pistol. He kept it concealed, waiting for the right moment. The photographer next to him was focused on Richardson, camera raised. No one was watching Shaklam.

Richardson continued her speech, her voice rising with passion. "Some will call us warmongers. Some will say we're too aggressive, too willing to use force. But I say we're realists. We understand the world as it is, not as we wish it to be."

She drew more cheers and more applause.

Shaklam drew the weapon slowly, keeping it low and concealed behind the reporter in front of him. He checked his line of sight. It was clear, with no obstructions.

He raised the pistol slightly, sighting along the barrel. Richardson's chest filled his vision. Center mass. Two shots to ensure a kill.

"We will not apologize for defending ourselves," Richardson said. "We will not apologize for protecting our children. We will not —"

Shaklam fired twice.

The suppressor muffled the shots, but the sound still registered. A sharp crack, barely audible over the crowd noise. The first shot caught Richardson high in the chest, just below the collarbone.

The second shot hit lower, near her heart.

Richardson collapsed, blood spewing onto the stage. Her aide screamed and rushed forward. Secret Service agents materialized from everywhere, weapons drawn, shouting commands.

The crowd erupted into chaos. People screamed and ran for the exits. Others dove under their seats. Parents grabbed their children and fled.

Shaklam moved quickly. He dropped the pistol and let it fall among the scattered press equipment where it clattered against a camera tripod. He turned and walked calmly toward the nearest exit, merging with the panicked crowd.

All around him, people shoved and pushed, desperate to escape. He moved with the flow, just another terrified citizen fleeing danger. He kept his face neutral, his movements unhurried. Running would draw attention.

A Secret Service agent grabbed his arm. "Sir, this way. We're evacuating the building."

"Thank God!" Shaklam said, and let the agent guide him toward a side exit.

Once outside, he broke away from the crowd and headed toward the van. Police sirens wailed in the distance, growing closer. Blue and red lights flashed from multiple directions. He had maybe ninety seconds before they locked down the entire area.

He walked quickly but didn't run. Running meant guilt. He was just a reporter who'd witnessed something terrible and needed to get to safety.

Two blocks. That's all he needed.

He reached the van, climbed inside, and slammed the door shut. His hands were steady as he picked up the game system and entered the return coordinates. The screen glowed, confirming the destination: Piney Woods, ammo shack.

Behind him, he could hear shouting and screaming, the chaos of an assassination scene. Emergency vehicles arrived. Officers were setting up perimeters. In a few minutes, they'd be questioning everyone who'd been in that convention center.

But he wouldn't be there to answer questions.

Shaklam pressed the teleport button and he disappeared. He felt the familiar sensation of displacement, of being unmade and remade somewhere else. The real world vanished.

When the world reformed, he was standing in the shack in the Piney Woods game environment. He was holding his game weapon now, the standard rifle all players started with.

He took a breath and moved toward the shack door. His WolfDen teammates were still out there somewhere, fighting the GhostWalkers. He needed to rejoin them and finish the match. *Act normal. Act like nothing had happened.*

He pushed open the door and stepped into the forest.

Gunfire erupted immediately.

Brie and Pete, positioned in the trees west of the shack, opened fire simultaneously. The first shot hit Shaklam in the shoulder, spinning his avatar around. The second caught him in the chest. The third struck his head, and his avatar dissolved into digital particles.

The game system announced the kill in a flat, automated voice: "WolfDen player eliminated. GhostWalkers achieve victory."

Brie got on the comm, her voice excited and breathless. "Holy shit. We got him. We won."

～

Joey pulled off his VR headset and grinned. "Good shooting. That's how you do it."

Tony high-fived him. "One and one. We're tied up."

Pete and Brie were celebrating their kills, replaying the final moments of the match.

None of them had any idea what had just happened.

Chapter Thirty-One
THE AFTERMATH

Missy and Sean sat at the kitchen table, a deck of cards spread between them and half-empty wine glasses within easy reach. They'd been playing gin rummy for the past hour, enjoying one of their rare quiet evenings at home.

When Joey and his friends walked in from the bedroom, their voices were still loud from whatever game session they just finished. Missy sat up straight and set her cards face down on the table.

"Hey, Mom. What's up?" Joey said, heading toward the refrigerator.

Sean held up his finger to silence them. His other hand reached for the remote and raised the volume on the TV. "Listen to this."

The newscaster's voice filled the kitchen, solemn and measured. "We'll all miss the acerbic wit and strong opinions of Senator Richardson. She was a beacon of reason and a strong voice against terrorism in this day of pacifism."

Joey stopped mid-stride, his hand still on the refrigerator door handle. Tony, Pete, and Brie gathered behind him, their attention drawn to the television mounted on the wall.

Sean paused the TV and turned in his chair to face them. His expression was grim, the kind of look he wore when bad news from work followed him home.

Missy's voice cracked as she spoke. "Oh my God. Somebody killed Senator Richardson."

For a moment, no one moved — or spoke.

Brie took a step back and opened her eyes wide. Her hand went to her mouth. "Did you say Richardson?"

"Yes, the Texas senator who was so opposed to being lenient on the terrorists. She's from Houston."

Joey glanced at Brie, then at Tony. Something passed between them, a look of recognition that Missy and Sean didn't catch.

"Oh my God, that's terrible," Brie said. She lowered her hand from her mouth. "Did they catch who did it?"

Sean clenched his fist on the table until his knuckles turned white. The wine glass shook slightly from the pressure. "Not yet. The shooter got away clean. Witnesses said he was seen getting in a van, then he was gone."

Missy reached across the table and placed her hand over Sean's fist. "They'll find him. They always do."

"Maybe," Sean said. But his tone suggested he wasn't so sure.

Tony moved closer to the TV, studying the paused image of the news broadcast. "Where did it happen?"

"The Houston Convention center," Sean said. "She was giving a speech at some business coalition luncheon. There were fifteen hundred people in attendance."

"And nobody saw the shooter?" Pete asked.

"They saw him," Sean said. "He had press credentials that blended right in with the reporters. By the time the Secret Service realized what happened, he was gone."

Joey pulled a chair out from the table and sat down. "That's crazy. I mean, how does someone just disappear like that?"

Sean shrugged. "That's what we'll have to figure out."

Brie shifted her weight from one foot to the other. Joey noticed the movement, the nervous energy she was barely containing. She tapped him on the back and gestured subtly toward the bedroom with her head.

Joey caught the signal and stood. "All right, guys. We're going back to practice. See you later."

Missy looked up from the table. "Aren't you going to listen to the rest of the news?"

"We're in the middle of tournament prep," Joey said. "We've got a break between matches, but we need to review strategy."

"Right now?" Missy gestured toward the TV. "A senator was just murdered, Joey. Take a few minutes to process that."

Tony spoke up. "We'll process it while we practice. Trust me, we're all shaken up about it, but us watching the news won't make a difference; us practicing will."

Sean studied the group. Something about their body language bothered him, though he couldn't put his finger on what. They seemed nervous, agitated in a way that didn't quite match the situation. "You kids knew who Senator Richardson was?"

"Sure," Joey said. "She was all over the news. It was hard to miss her."

"And you cared about her politics?"

Joey hesitated just a fraction too long. "Not really. I mean, we knew she was important. It's just shocking, that's all."

Sean nodded slowly. "All right. Go practice. But keep it down."

"Will do," Joey said.

Sean watched them go, his investigator's instincts firing warning signals he couldn't quite interpret.

When they were gone, Missy picked up her wine glass and took a long sip. "Those kids are hiding something."

"I know," Sean said. He reached for his own wine glass. "But right now, I've got bigger problems. Director Samuels is going to want a full briefing first thing tomorrow morning. This Richardson thing is going to blow up into a major investigation."

"You think it was terrorists?"

"It has to be. The method, the target, the clean escape. It's got all the hallmarks."

Missy set her glass down and reached for Sean's hand. "Just promise me you'll be careful. If they can get to a senator in a room full of people, they can get to anyone."

"I'll be careful," Sean said. But even as he said it, he was thinking about his kids in the next room, and the way they'd reacted to the news.

"Something about this whole situation didn't add up," he said, "And I intend to find out what it is."

Chapter Thirty-Two
BRIE'S CONFESSION

After they entered the bedroom, Joey took Brie aside and whispered, "What was that about? What's up?"

Brie checked that the door was closed before responding. "Remember I told you about the guy at the shack? He mentioned her."

"Mentioned who?"

"I heard him on the comm, and the person on the other end asked him if he got Richardson."

Tony moved closer, his face showing concern. "You think he meant the senator?"

"I don't know," Brie said. "But maybe we should tell your dad. I'm scared."

Joey paused a moment, scratching his head.

Tony's eyes widened. "Holy shit. Maybe that's how they did it."

"Did what?"

"How they killed the senator. They got the coordinates for where she'd be and entered them into the portal. Then they shot her and disappeared through the portal."

Brie moved closer to Joey and hugged him. "If they can do that, they can kill anyone."

"And if they killed her, they might try for the president," Tony said. "He's considered an enemy."

Joey pulled back from Brie. "We need to tell Dad."

Pete nodded. "Your dad needs to know."

Tony crossed his arms. "Fine, but we all need to go in there because Dad's not gonna believe any of it."

"Let's do it," Joey said.

In the kitchen, Missy and Sean were still watching the news when Joey and his friends entered. Brie hung back near the doorway.

"Can we talk a minute?" Joey asked.

Sean paused the TV and turned around. "It needs to be quick, bud. I'm probably going to catch hell over the senator being killed."

"We uh, we think—"

Tony stepped forward. "We know how Senator Richardson was killed. More importantly, we know who did it."

Sean chuckled. "Whoa, boys. I appreciate you trying to help, but that's a pretty bold statement. How would you know?"

Tony straightened up and spoke confidently. "Because it's the team we're fighting in the finals. They used a portal to teleport to other locations using GPS coordinates."

Sean laughed harder, and even Missy joined in. Sean stood and patted Tony on the back. "You realize what you're saying is impossible. I know technology has come a long way, but not this far."

Joey spoke hurriedly. "Brie saw one of them use it."

Brie kicked Joey in the leg and shot him a stern look. Sean stopped laughing and turned to Brie. "Tell me what you saw, Brie," Sean said patiently.

She glared at Joey, then folded her hands in front of her and looked straight at Mr. Lugullo. "I was guarding the shack when one of the WolfDen team entered. I took a bead on him, but before I shot, I heard him talking on his comm, and the person on the other end asked him if he got Richardson."

Sean pulled out a chair and gestured for Brie to sit. As she lowered herself onto the seat, his brows knit together. He slid a glass of water toward her. "Then what happened?"

Brie spoke more confidently. "I shot him after that."

Sean sipped his wine and nodded. "And that's it?"

"That's all I've got, sir."

Sean looked at each member of the team, his expression skeptical. The kitchen fell silent except for the hum of the refrigerator. Joey shifted his weight from one foot to the other, waiting for his father's response.

"Look," Sean finally said, "I know you want to help, but we need to focus on real things — things that can be tracked and run down as leads."

Tony shook his head. "I knew you wouldn't believe us, Dad. But what they're not telling you is that we tried it and did it ourselves."

Missy gasped, and Sean raised his eyebrows. "What?"

Tony nodded. "We presumed they used GPS coordinates, so we tried it. We went to the shack, entered GPS coordinates for outside our house, and like magic, we appeared there, right by the street."

Sean set his wine glass down carefully. "And you weren't smoking anything when you did this?"

Tony laughed. "Dad, you're with the FBI."

"Does that mean you wouldn't do it, or wouldn't say?"

"Exactly."

Sean leaned back in his chair and crossed his arms. "All right, I'll take this up with my team tomorrow."

Tony stared at his father. "You're not going to do anything, are you?"

"Of course I am, but I can't just go in there with a story like this. I need evidence, something concrete."

Tony nodded slowly, then took his phone out and moved to the center of the room. He pulled up the GPS coordinates, then turned to Brie. "Brie, can you go to the teleport site and use the coordinates I just texted you?"

Brie pulled her phone out and double-checked the GPS numbers. She looked at Tony, then at Sean, then back at Tony. "You're serious?"

"Dead serious."

She nodded and left the room. They heard the Joey's door close behind her.

Sean tilted his head to the side and raised his eyebrows. "What are you doing?"

"Showing you what you need to see."

Missy stood up from the table. "Tony, what's going on? Where did Brie go?"

"Just wait."

Sean glanced at his watch, then at Joey. "How long is this going to take?"

"Not long," Joey said.

The seconds ticked by. Sean checked his phone. Missy paced near the counter. Pete shifted uncomfortably by the doorway.

Then, without warning, a low humming sound filled the kitchen. The air in the center of the room shimmered, and suddenly Brie materialized right where Tony had been standing.

Missy gasped and stumbled backward, catching herself on the counter. Sean jumped up from his seat, knocking his chair over.

"What the hell," Sean said.

Tony grabbed a bottle of water from the fridge and handed it to Brie. She was breathing hard, her hands shaking slightly. "That's how they did it."

Sean stared at Brie, then at Tony, then back at Brie. His face had gone pale. "That's not possible."

"You just watched it happen," Tony said.

Missy moved closer, her hand over her mouth. "Brie, are you okay?"

Brie nodded and took a long drink of water. "I'm fine. Just a little dizzy."

Sean walked around Brie in a slow circle, as if inspecting her for signs of a trick. "This is real? This actually happened?"

"We've done it several times," Joey said. "That's how WolfDen has been beating everyone."

Sean picked up his chair and sat down heavily. He rubbed his face with both hands. "Okay. Okay, let me think."

"Dad," Tony said, "if they can do this in the game, and if they mentioned Richardson, then maybe—"

"Maybe they're doing it in real life," Sean finished. He looked up at his son. "But that would require technology that doesn't exist. At least, not that we know of."

"What if it does exist?" Brie asked quietly. "What if someone created it and we just don't know about it?"

Sean was quiet for a long moment. When he spoke again, his voice was different — sharper, more focused. This was his FBI voice. "Tell me everything. From the beginning. Every detail you remember about this portal system."

Joey pulled out a chair and sat down. "It started when we noticed WolfDen getting behind us without Tony seeing them. We couldn't figure out how they were doing it."

"Then I tracked one of them to an ammo shack," Brie continued. "There was a structure inside that looked like an old shack. He went in, pressed some buttons on a keypad, and disappeared."

"Just vanished?" Sean asked.

"Like he was never there."

Tony leaned against the counter. "We went back later to investigate and found a monitor with GPS coordinates and a keypad with preset buttons. Red, blue, green. Each one goes to a different location on the map."

"And you tested it?" Missy asked.

"We had to know if it was real," Pete said. "So Tony got the coordinates for our front yard and Brie entered them."

"Then we all went through together," Joey added. "We ended up exactly where we wanted to be. Right by the street, just like Tony said."

Sean pulled out his phone and started typing notes. "How many of these portal stations are there?"

"Only one that we've found," Tony said. "It's like a network across the whole map."

"And WolfDen knows about this?"

"They've been using it for months," Joey said. "That's how they've won five tournaments in a row. Nobody else figured it out until we did."

Sean finished typing and looked up. "And you said you heard them mention Richardson on the comm?"

Brie nodded. "The guy asked if he got Richardson. Those what he said."

"Did he say anything else?"

"Just that he was wounded and needed to return to base."

Sean stood up and started pacing. "If this technology exists in the game, someone had to program it. And if someone programmed it—"

"They might have built a real version," Tony said.

"Or the game is testing a prototype," Joey added.

Sean stopped pacing and looked at his family. "I need to make some calls. Tony, Joey, write down everything you know about this portal. Coordinates, button configurations, how the system works. Everything."

"What are you going to do?" Missy asked.

"I'm going to call the director. If there's even a chance this is connected to Richardson's assassination, we need to move on it now."

He headed toward his office, then stopped and turned back. "And kids? Good work. Seriously. If this pans out, you might have just cracked the case."

After Sean left, Missy sat down heavily. She looked at the spot where Brie had appeared and shook her head. "I can't believe what I just saw."

"None of us could at first," Pete said.

Brie set her water bottle down. "Mrs. Lugullo, are we in trouble?"

Missy looked at her, then smiled tiredly. "No, honey. You're not in trouble. You're heroes. Stupid, reckless heroes, but heroes nonetheless."

Tony grinned. "I'll take it."

Joey stood up. "Come on, let's go write everything down for Dad. The more detail we can give him, the better."

As they filed out of the kitchen, Brie grabbed Joey's arm. "You think your dad will really look into this?"

"Yeah, I do. You saw his face. That was his work mode kicking in."

"Good." She paused. "Because if WolfDen really killed the senator, they need to be stopped."

"They will be," Joey said. "One way or another."

Chapter Thirty-Three
PREPARING FOR A TOURNAMENT

The kids went back to Joey's room, and Sean poured another glass of wine. Missy leaned close and whispered, "How in God's name did that happen?"

"I don't know." Sean set the bottle down carefully, his hand not quite steady. "But at least I have something solid now."

"I'm worried."

Sean reached over and patted the back of Missy's hand. His fingers were cold despite the warmth of the kitchen. "I am too, but I'll check this out."

Missy pulled her hand back and wrapped both arms around herself. "Sean, if what they're saying is true—"

"I know."

"Senator Richardson was killed three days ago. If these people have access to this technology—"

"I know. I know." Sean took a long drink of wine. "I'll call Daniels as soon as I finish writing down everything the kids told us."

"Tonight?"

"Tonight." He stood and carried his glass to the sink. "This can't wait until morning."

Missy followed him and lowered her voice even more. "What if they come here? What if they know the kids figured it out?"

Sean turned to face her. "Then we'll deal with it. But right now, the best thing we can do is get this information to the Bureau and let them handle it."

"And the kids?"

"After this, the kids are done with it." Sean glanced toward the hallway where Joey's room was. "They've done their part. Now it's our turn."

In Joey's bedroom, Joey plopped on the sofa and Brie sat next to him. Pete and Tony took their usual beanbag seats.

Tony shook his head. "It'll take him a while to grasp what we showed him."

"We can't worry about that," Joey said. "We've got a game to prepare for."

Tony's face darkened. "Christ, Joey, stop being so selfish. We're talking about the someone's life — maybe even the president."

Pete leaned back in his beanbag. "Fuck the president. What'd he ever do for us?"

Brie turned to stare at Pete. "You can't be serious."

"What? I'm just saying—"

"You're just saying you don't care if someone gets assassinated because it doesn't affect you directly?" Brie's voice was sharp. "That's messed up, Pete."

Pete shrugged. "I didn't mean it like that."

"Then how did you mean it?"

Joey held up his hand. "All right, enough. Look, Tony's right that this is serious, and Pete's being an idiot.

"We told Dad we'd write down what we know, so let's do that, but then we have a tournament to win. So here's what we're going to do." He looked at each of them. "We write what we know, focus on winning the next game, then we'll see if we can help the president. Dad's handling the investigation side. That's his job, not ours."

Tony crossed his arms. "And if WolfDen knows we figured out their secret?"

"Then we beat them anyway," Brie said. "We've done it once. We can do it again."

Pete sat forward. "She's right. We know their tricks now. They don't have the advantage anymore."

Joey nodded. "Exactly. So we practice tonight, get some rest, and tomorrow we finish this."

Tony was quiet for a moment, then sighed. "Fine. But after we win, we tell Dad everything we know. Every detail."

"Deal," Joey said.

Brie stood and stretched. "I should probably head home. It's late, and I need to document what I saw, then clear my head before tomorrow."

"You sure?" Joey asked.

"Yeah. Besides, your parents probably need some space to process what just happened."

Joey walked her to the door. In the hallway, she turned to face him. "Your dad's going to take this seriously, right?"

"You saw his expression when you appeared."

"I know, but sometimes adults say they'll do something and then—"

"He'll do it," Joey said firmly. "My dad's a lot of things, but he's not a liar."

Brie nodded. "Okay. I trust you."

After she left, Joey returned to his room. Tony and Pete were already reviewing footage from their last game against WolfDen.

"Look at this part," Tony said, pointing at the screen. "Right here, the guy pauses before entering the shack. He's checking something."

"Coordinates," Pete said. "He's making sure he's got the right ones entered."

Joey leaned over to watch. "How long does he pause?"

"Three seconds. Maybe four."

"That's our window," Joey said. "If we can catch them in that pause, we can take them out before they teleport."

Tony rewound the footage. "But we'd have to know when they're at the shack."

"We can predict it," Brie's voice came from the doorway. They all turned to see her standing there. "Sorry, I forgot my phone."

She crossed the room and picked up her phone from the couch, but instead of leaving, she sat back down. "I was thinking about their pattern on the way out. There's got to be a pattern."

"There is," Tony said. "Every time they use the portal, even if it's to teleport behind another team, they disperse in all directions as soon as they spawn. And two of them *always* head toward the shack, then when they reach it, one of the team keeps going and the other stays behind."

"Right. Which means if we control the shack, we can force them into predictable movements."

Joey thought about it. "We'd need to stay together and surround the shack. It could be risky."

"Too risky," Pete said. "If they hit with their full team, we might be swamped."

"Not if we're coordinated," Brie said. "We can catch them in a crossfire."

Tony grinned. "I like it. It's aggressive."

"It's dangerous," Pete said.

"So is doing nothing," Joey said. "WolfDen's not going to change their strategy. They're too confident. That makes them predictable."

He stood up and grabbed a marker, then started drawing on the whiteboard mounted on his wall. "Here's how we do it. Tony, you're on the north side with Pete. Brie and I take the west side."

"No good," Tony said. "They usually spawn north of the shack. We should be positioned on both flanks, so Pete and I on the east side, and you and Brie on the west."

Brie nodded. "That makes more sense. It's the best way to catch them in a crossfire."

Pete nodded. "Got it."

They spent the next two hours running scenarios, testing different approaches, refining the plan. By the time they finished, it was past two in the morning.

Pete yawned and stood up. "I'm done. I can't think anymore."

"Yeah, we should all get some sleep," Joey said. "Tomorrow's the big one."

After Pete left, Tony went to Tony's room and stood by the door. "You really think we can beat them?"

"I know we can," Tony said. "We're better than they are. We just didn't know it until now."

Joey smiled. "When did you become so confident?"

"When Brie joined the team."

He paused. "She's good for you, you know. She keeps you honest."

Joey threw a pillow at him. "Get out of here."

"Turn off the light when you leave, asshole."

Tony lay on his bed and stared at the ceiling. His mind raced with strategies, contingencies, and what-ifs. Tomorrow wasn't just about winning a game anymore. It was about proving they could stand up to WolfDen. And about showing that the GhostWalkers weren't just lucky kids who stumbled onto a secret.

Joey's phone buzzed. A text from Brie: *I can't sleep. I'm too wired.*

He typed back: *Same here. Just keep thinking about tomorrow. We're going to win.*

I know, so get some rest. We need you sharp.

Joey smiled. *Yes ma'am.*

He set his phone aside and closed his eyes.

The next morning, Joey woke to sunlight streaming through his window. He checked his phone. Ten AM. He'd slept for seven hours which was much more than he expected.

There was a text from Tony: *Dad left early for work. He said he's following up on what we told him.*

Joey typed back: *Good. See you soon.*

He got up and headed to the kitchen. His mother was sitting at the table with her laptop open, a cup of coffee in her hand.

"Morning," Joey said.

"Good morning. How did you sleep?"

"Better than I thought I would." He poured himself coffee. "Is Dad gone?"

"He left at six. He didn't want to wake you, but said he'd call if he had questions." Missy closed her laptop. "Joey, what you kids showed us last night—"

"I know, Mom. You're worried."

"This isn't a game anymore. If what you're saying is true, if these people really killed Senator Richardson, then you're involved in something very dangerous."

Joey sat down across from her. "We're just playing a tournament. That's all."

"Your father seems to think otherwise."

"What did he say?"

Missy was quiet for a moment. "He said he's going to have agents monitor your game tonight. Just in case."

"In case of what?"

"In case WolfDen is more than just a gaming team."

Joey felt a chill run down his spine. "You think they'd come after us?"

"I don't know. But your father's not taking any chances." She reached across the table and squeezed his hand. "Be careful tonight. Please."

"I will, Mom. I promise."

That afternoon, the team gathered at Joey's house. The mood was different from before. Everything was more serious and focused.

Tony was the first to sit down. He was followed by Pete, then Brie. They assembled without the usual joking around.

"We can't afford to lose this one," Tony said.

"We won't," Brie said.

Pete nodded. "I'm ready."

Joey looked at each of them. "Time to rock 'n' roll. This is only another practice game, but it's a chance to show them who they're facing."

"It's more than that," Tony said. "If WolfDen really is involved in Richardson's assassination, we need to win. We need to prove they're not invincible."

"Then let's prove it," Brie said.

They spent the next three hours running drills, perfecting their timing, and making sure everyone knew their role. When they finally took a break, Joey checked the tournament app.

Game three starts in two hours.

"Everyone take a break," Joey said. "Eat something, hydrate, clear your heads. When we come back, we go in ready to end this."

As the others filed out, Brie stayed behind. She closed the door and turned to Joey. "Are you nervous?"

"Yeah. You?"

"Terrified."

Joey smiled. "At least we're honest."

"That's what I like about you," Brie said. "You don't pretend to be something you're not."

"Is that a compliment?"

"Take it however you want." She moved closer. "But whatever happens tonight, I'm glad I joined the team."

"Me too."

They stood there for a moment, neither one speaking. Then Brie reached out and squeezed his hand.

"Let's win this thing," she said.

"Yeah. Let's do it."

Chapter Thirty-Four
A VISIT TO DEATHMASTER

San Francisco

Sean was shown into Rick Tilson's office by a receptionist who disappeared the moment she opened the door. The office was impressive, all mahogany and leather with floor-to-ceiling windows. Tilson sat behind a large desk that probably cost more than Sean's annual salary.

A bright light shone through the corner windows, forcing Sean to shield his eyes. The positioning was deliberate, a ploy to give Rick the edge. Tilson wanted visitors backlit, and at a disadvantage. Sean moved to a plush chair with his back facing the windows, eliminating the problem.

Tilson was younger than Sean had expected, maybe early forties, with the kind of tan that came from yacht weekends and the confidence that came from having more money than sense. He wore an expensive suit and a watch that could have funded a small country.

"What can I do for you, Agent Lugullo?" Tilson asked, his voice smooth and practiced.

Sean shifted in his seat to get comfortable. This wasn't going to be easy. "I have an odd request, Mr. Tilson. I need to know if your game is capable of teleporting people from place to place based on GPS coordinates. And I don't mean characters. I mean real people."

Rick laughed heartily, the sound echoing off the high ceiling. "I know you didn't come all this way to make me laugh, but you realize that question is preposterous."

Sean stared intently and leaned forward. His expression didn't change. "You're right that I didn't come here to make you laugh, but you didn't answer the question."

The smile vanished from Rick's face like someone had flipped a switch. He leaned forward, focusing on Sean with new intensity. The casual CEO persona disappeared, replaced by something harder, more calculating.

"I don't respond to questions of a proprietary nature without my lawyer," Rick said carefully. "If you like, I can get him here within moments."

Rick stood and walked toward the door, but Sean was faster. He grabbed Rick's jacket and pulled him back, not roughly but firmly enough to make his point.

"Just call him on the phone," Sean said, his voice commanding.

"He doesn't always answer."

Sean looked up at Rick and smiled sardonically. "I'm sure he will for the CEO. Call."

Rick's jaw tightened, but he returned to his desk and picked up the phone. He pressed a button. "Sid? I need you in my office. Now." He hung up without waiting for a response.

While they waited, Sean studied Rick. The man had gone pale when Sean mentioned teleportation. Not the reaction of someone hearing an absurd question. More like the reaction of someone whose secret had just been exposed.

"Why are you hesitant to tell me what I need to know?" Sean asked.

"Whenever something has the potential to adversely affect sales, I'm reluctant," Rick said.

Before Sean could respond, the door opened and a man walked in. Sid Ryczitz looked to be in his fifties, with the bearing of an attorney who'd spent decades protecting corporate interests. He wore a dark suit and carried a leather briefcase. His expression was serious and professional, giving nothing away.

"Good morning, gentlemen," Sid said. "How may I be of help?"

"Sean is an FBI agent," Rick said, "and he would like to know about our proprietary technology in the new system."

Sean sat up straight. "Only as it pertains to a specific feature."

Sid leaned close to Rick and whispered in his ear. Rick whispered back. Sean watched the exchange, frustrated. He could see Sid shaking his head slightly, Rick arguing quietly. After a moment, they separated.

"I'm afraid we can't oblige," Sid said. "If you are able to obtain a warrant, I'm sure we could help."

Sean stood, hiding his disappointment behind a neutral expression. He'd expected this, but he'd hoped the direct approach might work. Clearly, Tilson had something to hide.

"And I'm sure we can arrange a warrant," Sean said.

He headed toward the door but turned around before he left. Rick and Sid were watching him, waiting to see if he'd leave quietly.

"If we have to get a warrant," Sean said, "be assured the papers will know when it's served."

Sid's expression hardened. "I take that as a threat."

"As you should. Good day, gentlemen."

Sean walked out, pulling the door closed behind him. The receptionist looked up nervously as he passed, clearly having heard raised voices. Sean gave her a polite nod and headed for the elevator.

In the hallway, he pulled out his phone and called Sorenson.

"I need you to start warrant paperwork for DeathMaster headquarters," Sean said when Sorenson answered. "Everything. Their technology, their code, their communications. All of it."

"What did you find?" Sorenson asked.

"They're hiding something. Tilson practically admitted it. He wouldn't answer a direct question without his lawyer, and the lawyer shut him down immediately."

"That's not necessarily proof of anything illegal."

"No, but it's proof they're scared. And scared companies make mistakes." Sean pressed the elevator button. "Get the warrant started. I'll work on getting a judge to sign it."

"You think they'll destroy evidence?"

"I think if they have teleportation technology and they're letting it be used for terrorism, they'll do whatever it takes to keep it secret." The elevator doors opened. "Which means we need to move fast."

After Sean hung up, he stood in the elevator as it descended, thinking about Rick's reaction. The man had been genuinely surprised by the question. But not because it was absurd. Because Sean knew about it.

Which meant the technology existed. And if it existed, WolfDen had access to it. And if WolfDen had access to it, they could strike anywhere, anytime, without warning.

The elevator reached the ground floor. Sean walked through the gleaming lobby of DeathMaster headquarters, past the elaborate displays showing off their most popular games. Young people clustered around demo stations, laughing and competing. They had no idea that the game they were playing might be connected to terrorism.

Outside, Sean got in his car and sat for a moment. His phone buzzed with a text from Tony: *How did it go?*

Sean typed back: *Getting a warrant. They're hiding something.*

I knew it.

Stay at the house. Don't go anywhere.

We won't.

Sean started the car and pulled out of the parking lot. In his rearview mirror, he could see the DeathMaster building, all glass and steel and corporate success. Somewhere in there, someone knew exactly how the terrorists were teleporting. Someone had built that technology, programmed it, and tested it.

And Sean was going to find out who.

Chapter Thirty-Five
A FAILED ATTEMPT

The GhostWalkers immediately split up. Tony and Pete headed east under the cover of heavy foliage. Brie and Joey stayed put and settled in on the west side, waiting for an attack from either the north or south.

Cyrus and his WolfDen team appeared in the north and headed south. Cyrus tapped Shaklam on the back and pointed south. "Teleport behind them and take potshots, but don't get close enough to be hit." He paused. "The rest of you stay with me. We'll advance slowly and hit them when they least expect it." Another pause. "And nobody make noise."

Cyrus and two others got on their bellies and crawled south slowly. Meanwhile, Shaklam teleported far south to the GhostWalkers' rear and took a position behind a large boulder. He made sure to snap a few branches to attract their attention.

Joey heard the noise. "Pete, they're coming up from the south."

Pete and Tony moved carefully through the trees. Pete advanced south, toward the sound Joey heard, his weapon raised.

Cyrus saw Tony and Pete moving south. "Keep it up, Shaklam, it's working."

Shaklam dashed to the east side of the shack, seeking cover behind a large pine.

Pete and Tony fired at him. They missed, but their action gave Cyrus and his team time to advance.

The WolfDen team moved slowly, switching direction and crawling through the underbrush toward Joey and Brie. When they got close enough, they opened fire.

Cyrus's first shot hit Joey in the back of the head. He stumbled forward and collapsed. Rizwan took out Brie with two chest shots, and she dropped beside Joey. Tony scrambled for cover, but a protruding branch knocked his headphones loose. Then WolfDen tossed grenades, and the explosions lit up the screen. They opened fire with automatics, the noise deafening even through the game's audio dampening feature.

Tony took cover behind a fallen log and searched frantically for his headphones. He shook his head to clear it, but the noise combined with flashing lights was overwhelming. He covered his ears with his hands and crawled toward an enclave of rocks.

Rizwan and Sandof shifted directions and, after spotting Tony, advanced toward him. When they closed in, they took him out with a headshot. The only GhostWalker remaining was Pete.

Shaklam advanced until he had Pete in his sights. Pete ran for cover, weaving between trees, but Shaklam tracked him perfectly and took him out with two quick shots.

The screen flashed: WOLFDEN WINS.

In Joey's bedroom, Pete stared at Tony. "What the hell was that about?"

Tony lowered his head and shrugged. "I froze."

"No shit you froze."

"Enough, Pete," Joey said. "Nobody said anything when you screwed up — twice."

Pete turned on him. "This is different. We had them. We were in position, we knew their strategy, and Tony just—"

"I said enough." Joey's voice was sharp.

The room went quiet. Brie sat on the couch, her arms crossed, staring at the floor. Tony remained in his beanbag, not looking at anyone.

Finally, Brie spoke but her tone was consoling, not derogatory. "What happened out there, Tony? For real."

Tony took a deep breath. "The headphones came off and everything hit at once. The grenades, the gunfire, the lights. I couldn't think straight."

"You panicked," Pete said.

"Yeah. I panicked." Tony looked up, meeting Pete's eyes. "Happy now?"

"No, I'm not happy. We just lost the game because you couldn't handle some noise."

Joey stood up. "That's enough. Both of you."

"He's right, though," Tony said quietly. "I cost us the game."

Brie uncrossed her arms and leaned forward. "It wasn't just you. I got caught in the open. Joey didn't watch his six. We all made mistakes."

"But mine was the biggest," Tony said.

Joey sat back down. "Look, we lost. It sucks. But we made it to the finals against the best team in the league. That's something."

"*Something* isn't not good enough," Pete said. "We should have won."

"But we didn't." Joey looked at each of them. "So now what? We beat ourselves up over it, or we figure out what went wrong and fix it for next time?"

Tony nodded slowly.

"Then we learn from this and move on." Joey stood and walked to the window. "WolfDen's good. Better than we gave them credit for. But we hung with them. That means something."

Brie joined him at the window. "Is your dad still looking into the Richardson thing?"

"I assume so. I haven't heard from him yet."

"That's more important than the tournament anyway," Tony said.

Joey turned around. "Maybe. But right now, all we can control is how we respond to this loss."

Pete stood and stretched. "I need to clear my head. I'm gonna take off."

After Pete left, Tony looked at Joey and Brie. "You think he's mad at me?"

"He's mad at himself," Brie said. "He just doesn't know it yet."

"She's right," Joey said. "Give him some time. He'll come around."

Tony headed to his room. "I should go too. I need to figure out what went wrong, and make sure the headphones don't come loose next time."

After Tony left, Joey and Brie sat together on the couch. Neither spoke for several minutes.

Finally, Brie broke the silence. "Are you okay?"

"Yeah. Disappointed, but okay."

"Me too." She leaned back against the cushions. "Do you think we'll get another shot at them in the tournament?"

Joey considered it. "I don't know. It depends on if the other teams' rankings. The last time I checked, we were way ahead, so I'm guessing we're still ranked number two."

Joey's phone buzzed. It was a text from his father: *Need to talk. Coming home early.*

He showed it to Brie. "It looks like we're about to find out what he learned."

"Should I stay?"

"If you want."

Brie gave it thought, but only for a moment. "I think I want to."

Twenty minutes later the front door opened, and Sean's footsteps came down the hallway, then he appeared in the doorway of Joey's room.

"We need to talk," Sean said. "And get Tony and Pete back here."

Chapter Thirty-Six
ATTEMPTED MURDER

Joey answered a knock at the door and found Ritchie standing on the porch.

"Mind if I come in and watch?"

"Hell no. I don't know if you heard, but we got our asses kicked last night. Maybe you'll see something that will help."

"I doubt it, but I'll try."

Joey stepped aside to let him in. "This is another practice game, Ritchie. We get three before the tournament game."

In Joey's bedroom, Ritchie plopped on a beanbag while Joey sat on the sofa.

"Look who's here," Brie said, smiling.

"Hey, Ritchie," Tony called out.

"Ritchie," Pete nodded.

Brie walked over and hugged him. "Glad you're here. We need all the help we can get."

Everyone took their seats. Joey pulled a vape from his pocket and fired it up. Billows of smoke filled the room. Pete inhaled deeply, breathing in the smoke, then he rolled over and reached out his hand. "Lend me a vape."

"You need to buy your own," Joey said.

"As soon as we beat WolfDen, I will."

Tony shook his head. "You mean *if* we beat WolfDen. And open the damn windows if you're gonna smoke those things."

"You can't even smell them," Pete said.

"Maybe *you* can't, but I can."

Brie sat up straight, her eyes showing excitement. "I have an idea for the next game."

Pete smirked. "I hope it doesn't involve Tony."

"It won't happen again," Tony said quietly.

Tony started creeping toward the window. Joey watched him, confused.

"What the hell are you doing?" Joey asked.

"Shh. I heard something outside."

"I didn't hear anything," Pete said.

"Me neither," Joey added.

"I did."

Tony pulled the curtains aside, but just barely. He peered out into the darkness, scanning the front yard. After a long moment, he let the curtain fall back. "Guess it was nothing."

He went back to his seat, but something in his posture remained tense.

Shaklam leaned forward and spoke to the driver of the van. "Pull up slowly so they don't hear anything."

"I don't want to risk them seeing us."

"Don't worry about that. Just park across the street, and I'll take it from there."

"If you say so, just tell me when to stop. I'll wait there for you to finish."

"Stop here," Shaklam said. "It shouldn't take me more than a few minutes."

Inside Joey's bedroom, Pete moved next to the window and blew smoke outside after each drag. The night was quiet except for the distant sound of traffic. Then a low rumble hummed close by. Pete leaned forward and pressed his palms against the windowsill.

"Hey, y'all," he whispered. "Some guy just got out of a van, and he's sneaking across the front lawn. It looks like he's holding something in his hand too."

Tony crawled to the window, pulled the curtains aside, and peeked out. His body went rigid.

"Hand me the pellet gun, Joey."

"What the hell for?"

"Just give it to me. Quick!"

The urgency in Tony's voice made Joey move. He grabbed the gun from his closet, loaded it, and handed it to Tony.

"Brie, hold the curtain open just like I am so I can use both hands," Tony said.

"Should we call your dad?" Pete asked, his voice tight.

"Not yet."

Through the window, they watched the man stretch his hand out and raise it slightly.

"He's got something in his hand," Tony said.

The man lit a match and moved it toward what he was holding. In the brief flare of light, Tony saw what it was.

"It's a goddamn firebomb!"

Tony narrowed his eyes and focused. He zeroed in on the bottle in the man's hand until it was all he could see. His finger tightened on the trigger. He took a breath, held it, and squeezed.

The pellet hit the bottle dead center. Glass shattered, dousing the man with fluid. The match ignited it instantly. Flames covered the man's body and he screamed. The sound was terrible, piercing the quiet night.

The van parked on the street sped off, tires squealing. It turned at the first corner and disappeared.

"Christ, what the hell?" Joey said, jumping to his feet.

"They were trying to bomb us!" Pete shouted.

Tony raised the window, and he and the others climbed outside and ran to the body. The man's clothes were still on fire, but the screaming had stopped. He wasn't moving at all.

Ritchie moved close but had to step back because of the heat. "He's lucky he's dead or I'd have killed him worse."

Tony shot Ritchie a questioning look. "You know that makes no sense."

Just then, Sean and Missy ran out the front door. Sean took in the scene, his FBI training kicking in immediately.

"What the hell is going on?" He demanded.

Tony pointed to the man on the ground. "He tried to firebomb the house, so I shot his bottle."

Missy gasped, her hand flying to her mouth. "Oh my God! Call an ambulance."

"He's dead, Mom," Tony said, his voice flat.

Sean was already pulling out his cell phone. He dialed quickly, his eyes never leaving the burning body. "Connect me with Sorenson."

He waited, then spoke rapidly. "This is Lugullo. I need a full response team at my home address immediately. Attempted firebombing. One suspect down, deceased. Second suspect fled in a van, no plates observed." He paused, listening. "Yes, I'm sure. My son neutralized the threat with a pellet gun."

Missy wrapped her arms around herself, shivering despite the warm night. "Sean, the kids—"

"I know." He turned to Joey and the others. "Everyone inside. Don't touch anything, don't talk to anyone until I say so."

"But Dad—"

"Inside, Joey. Now!"

The tone left no room for argument. They filed back toward the house, but Joey glanced back at the body. The flames were dying down now, revealing charred clothing and blackened skin.

Brie grabbed his arm. "Come on. Don't look."

Inside, they gathered in the living room. Tony sat on the couch, staring at his hands. They were shaking slightly.

"You okay?" Brie asked quietly.

"I killed him."

"You saved us," Joey said. "If you hadn't shot that bottle —"

"I know what would have happened." Tony looked up. "But I still killed him."

Ritchie sat next to Tony. "You did what you had to do, man. That guy was gonna burn the house down with all of us in it."

Pete paced near the window. "Why would someone try to firebomb us?"

"WolfDen," Brie said. The room went quiet. "It had to be. We figured out their secret and told your dad about Richardson. They must have found out somehow, and now they're trying to silence us."

Joey felt his stomach drop. "If they know we told —"

"They'll try again," Pete said.

Outside, sirens wailed in the distance, growing louder. Red and blue lights began to flash through the windows.

Sean came back inside, his face grim. "The FBI's on the way. Local PD will secure the scene. Nobody goes outside, nobody talks to anyone except federal agents. Understood?"

They all nodded.

"I'll wait for them on the porch."

Sean sat on the porch and gulped down his coffee as he waited for the agent to arrive. A car pulled to the curb and Agent Sorenson, a tall man in his late thirties, walked toward the house. He stood as rigid as a telephone pole when he greeted Sean.

"I was expecting you a while ago," Sean said.

"We had a busy night, sir."

"I don't know why this happened. I'll leave that to you, but be thorough. These are my kids."

Sean and Sorenson walked to the body, which still lay in the front yard. Sorenson knelt next to it and examined it. The surrounding grass was burnt and blackened.

"What happened?" Sorenson asked.

"My kids heard a noise outside, and when they looked, this guy was lighting a Molotov cocktail. My youngest son shot the glass with his pellet gun, and it exploded."

"Hell of a shot."

Sean nodded. "He's a crack shot in both the real world and the game he plays, but I'd prefer it if he's not in the report. If you have to, say it was me who did it. I'll take the heat."

"I'll see what I can do."

"I'm most concerned about the man's identity. If we find that out, maybe we can learn why he did this."

Sorenson wore a somber expression as he nodded. "I can only imagine, sir. I've got kids myself, but don't worry, we'll get right on it."

"In the meantime, see if you can get a team up here to watch the house in case they try it again."

Agent Sorenson pulled out his phone. "I'm calling the coroner now."

Missy went to Tony with a blanket and wrapped it around his shoulders. "You're in shock, honey. Just breathe."

"Mom, I'm fine."

"You're not fine. You just killed someone. That's not fine."

Tony didn't argue.

Sean's phone rang as he came inside. He answered it, listened, then his expression darkened. "When? ... I see ... Yes, they're all here ... Understood."

He hung up and looked at the kids. "That was Sorenson. They found the van two miles from here but it was abandoned. They're running prints now, but he said something else." Sean paused. "Three hours ago, there was an attempted breach at another senator's house, but the FBI stopped it."

"What?" Joey said.

"I believe you're targets now. All of you, so everything you do will be monitored."

Ritchie's face went white. "My mom's gonna freak out if she hears about this."

"I'll talk to your parents, Ritchie. Yours too, Pete. I think it would be better if you both stayed here until this mess is over."

"You want us to stay here? Pete asked.

"I do, Pete. And you too, Brie. We have an extra bedroom you can use, and I'll talk to your mother and explain the situation."

"What about the tournament?" Tony asked.

Sean stared at him. "Are you serious? Someone just tried to burn down our house."

"These are the finals, Dad. If we don't show up, we forfeit."

"I don't care about a video game right now. I care about keeping you alive."

"But if WolfDen is behind this," Brie said, "then forfeiting is exactly what they want. They win by default, and nobody investigates them further."

Sean considered what she said. "That's a good point, but it doesn't change the fact that you're all in danger."

"Do whatever you need to do," Joey said. "But let us play."

"Absolutely not."

"Dad, listen —"

"I said no, Joey. This isn't up for debate."

Outside, tires screeched as multiple vehicles pulled up to the house. Car doors slammed. Heavy footsteps approached.

Sean went to the door and looked through the peephole, then unlocked it. Six FBI agents entered, all wearing tactical vests and carrying weapons. Sorenson, who had been there earlier, led them.

"Lugullo," Sorenson said, nodding at Sean. "We've secured the perimeter. A crime scene unit is processing the body now."

"It looks like you've got enough men here now," Tony said. "I guess we can play."

Chapter Thirty-Seven
SEAN'S REPORT

Sean arrived early and headed to Director Samuels' office. The space dwarfed Sean's own workspace and was far better organized. Commendations hung on the side wall, and aw enforcement texts and other books filled mahogany shelves on the back wall. Samuels sat behind a large oak desk, reviewing a file.

"Come in, Lugullo," Samuels said without looking up.

Sean entered and closed the door behind him. "Don't mean to disturb you, sir, but I have a few things to discuss."

Samuels set the file aside and gestured to the chair across from him. "Sit."

Sean sat down and shifted in his seat, fidgeting with his hands. He'd rehearsed this conversation a dozen times on the drive in, but now that he was here, the words felt ridiculous.

"My kids play this wildly popular game called —"

"I know which one," Samuels said. "The war game. DeathMaster or something like that."

Sean nodded. "While they were playing, one of them saw an enemy player enter a structure, then disappear — simply disappear. But before he did, he was on a comm call with the apparent team leader. A member of my son's team heard him ask if he got 'Richardson' yet."

Director Samuels leaned forward, his expression sharpening. "Richardson? He said that?"

"Yes, sir. And both my kids and the other team members back her up." Sean paused. "Not to mention, sir, the other night, a man we've identified as a known terrorist tried firebombing our house. If it wasn't for my son being a crack shot, he would have succeeded."

Samuels narrowed his eyes and stared at Sean. "And you believe this?"

"I have no choice but to believe. I saw the man in my front yard. He was holding a firebomb. And we have since identified him as a terrorist from Syria." Sean cleared his throat. "That same night, uh, one of the team ..."

Director Samuels glanced at the clock on the wall. "Get on with it, Lugullo."

"I saw a team member teleport into my kitchen."

Samuels stopped everything he was doing and stared. "You what?"

"She left the room, accessed the game system, then reappeared in the kitchen. Right in front of me, my wife, and the rest of the team."

Samuels slapped his palm onto the desktop. "I find it impossible to believe, Lugullo, but if it's enough for you to come see me and declare it's true, then it's enough for us to pursue." He paused. "Put a few teams together and assign them to everywhere the president goes. And get in touch with Agent Collins from the Secret Service. We need to coordinate with them."

"One more thing, sir. About the senator's funeral —"

"Get with Collins. The Secret Service has authority over the president's protection."

Samuels picked up his phone. "Lugullo, if this pans out the way I think it might, we're looking at technology that could change everything. Warfare, intelligence, everything. I want a full report on my desk by end of day."

"Yes, sir."

Sean stood to leave, but Samuels stopped him. "And Lugullo? Keep your kids close. If these people are willing to firebomb your house, they won't stop there."

"Already done, sir. They're under protective surveillance."

"Good. Now get me that report."

Sean left the office, his mind racing. As he walked back to his desk, he pulled out his phone and texted Joey: *How are the new guests?*

The response came quickly: *If you mean the prison you created — boring. When are they leaving?*

Soon. Stay put.

Sean sat at his desk and stared at his computer screen. The cursor blinked at him from a blank document. *Full report by end of day. Where do I even start?*

He typed the title: INVESTIGATION into POSSIBLE TELEPORTATION TECHNOLOGY and CONNECTION TO RICHARDSON ASSASSINATION

Then he stopped. After reading it, it sounded insane.

His phone rang.

"Lugullo, we've got an ID on your firebomber," Sorenson said. "His name's Rashid Al-Mansour. He's a Syrian national, and a known associate of several terrorist cells. But here's the interesting part — he entered the country three years ago on a student visa, and he's been studying Gaming Technology at MIT."

Sean's blood ran cold. "Gaming technology?"

"Yeah. Weird coincidence, right?"

"There are no coincidences in this business." Sean grabbed a pen and started taking notes. "What else?"

"We're running down his contacts now. But we found high-end equipment at his apartment: GPS systems, quantum processors, things we can't even identify yet. Our tech guys are analyzing it now."

"Keep me posted. And just to be safe, double the surveillance on my house."

"Consider it done."

Sean hung up and returned to his report. His fingers flew across the keyboard now. Gaming technology. Teleportation. Richardson. It was all connected.

He just had to prove it before someone else got killed.

Chapter Thirty-Eight
A KEY PRACTICE

That night, Brie entered Joey's bedroom and immediately turned on the fan. "Joey, you need to clean this once in a while. It smells like a stinky old pool room in here."

"It's not all me," Joey said from the couch. "Talk to Pete and Ritchie too."

Brie walked over and sat down. "You ready for this?"

"It's the next to the last practice before game six, and we can't afford to lose — which means you have to hold your own."

Brie leaned on the arm of the couch, kicked her long legs up, and rested them on Joey's lap. "Don't worry about me holding my own. I handle you, don't I?"

Joey smiled despite himself. "That's debatable."

Tony entered with Pete and Ritchie behind him. Two FBI agents stood in the hallway, watching.

"You guys about ready?" Tony asked.

"Yeah." Joey gently moved Brie's legs and stood up. "Let's do this."

They logged into the game. The screen flashed: Urban Sprawl — Night.

The GhostWalkers entered the game and immediately sought cover in the high grass close to the entrance. Tony crawled forward and squeezed between the other team members.

"Remember to be quiet," he whispered through the comm. "Kicking a can or stepping on broken glass could get us killed."

The rest of them gave the thumbs-up and prepared to advance.

The GhostWalker team crept forward while remaining crouched. They moved quietly from one dumpster to another, seeking cover in hidden alcoves in between. The urban landscape was a maze of destroyed buildings, abandoned vehicles, and debris-strewn streets.

Joey led the way, scanning for movement. Behind him, Brie kept her weapon ready, covering their rear. Pete and Tony flanked them on either side, moving in coordinated steps.

They headed south and continued advancing into the inner sections of the cityscape, using burnt-out buildings and freeway ramps to conceal themselves. The night made visibility difficult, but it also provided cover.

After a few hundred yards, they approached several empty, bombed-out buildings. Tony held up a closed fist and pointed south.

"They're not far," he whispered.

Joey could hear them now — faint footsteps, the creak of equipment. WolfDen was close.

The team took position. Joey and Brie ducked behind a concrete barrier. Tony climbed to a second-story window, his sniper rifle ready. Pete found cover behind an overturned car.

WolfDen approached, looking in all directions. There were four of them — Cyrus, Farouz, Rizwan, and Sandof. They moved cautiously, holding their weapons ready as they swept the area.

The GhostWalkers waited. Thirty yards. Twenty. Fifteen.

Tony gave the signal and everyone fired at once.

The coordinated attack caught WolfDen completely off guard. Rizwan went down immediately, hit by three shots from different angles. Sandof tried to run but Pete tracked him and took him out.

Cyrus and Farouz dove for cover, returning fire. Bullets pinged off the concrete barrier where Joey and Brie hid.

"They're splitting up," Tony said through the comm. "I've got one going east and one west."

"Pete, take the one going east," Joey said. "Brie and I will get the one headed west."

"Copy that."

Joey and Brie moved quickly through the ruins, tracking their prey. They could hear him ahead, his footsteps echoing off the broken walls.

"He's heading for the western border," Brie said.

"Not if we get there first."

They sprinted forward, abandoning stealth for speed. The border was fifty yards ahead, on the other side of an abandoned railway station.

Cyrus reached it first and disappeared inside.

"Damn it," Joey said.

Brie smiled. "I know where he's going."

"How?"

"There's only one exit from here that he can use." Brie got on the mic. "Tony, Pete, we need to cut him off. He'll be exiting the old railway station on the east side."

"On it," Tony said.

"I'll meet you there," Pete said. "I just took out my target."

They converged on the extraction point from three different angles. When Cyrus exited, he found himself surrounded.

He raised his hands slowly, then suddenly threw a flashbang.

Joey fired blindly, spraying the area. When his vision cleared, Cyrus was down but not dead.

Joey, Brie, and Tony walked forward slowly. When they arrived at the site, Cyrus's body lay on the ground.

"Congratulations," he said.

The screen flashed: GHOSTWALKERS WIN.

Joey and Tony joined their parents at the table for dinner.

"I heard you won the game today," Sean said.

"Yeah, and you should have seen the WolfDen leader. You'd never know he was the competition," Tony said. "When we beat them, he congratulated us as if he was our friend."

"Maybe you're wrong about them being the ones who shot Richardson."

Tony shook his head and spoke with conviction. "No, they did it, Dad. And I'm betting they target the president next."

"We'll find out. I'm going to D.C. tomorrow to meet with the Secret Service."

Tony sipped a glass of water, then spoke in a somber voice. "The Secret Service won't be able to protect him from these people."

"Your team beat them several times."

"We're used to fighting them, and I knew what to expect. I figured out their strategies, but even with that, they've beaten us an equal number of times.

"I'll let them know."

After dinner, Joey and Tony cleared the table, then retired to their rooms.

Chapter Thirty-Nine
THE DECOY

Sean passed through the security checkpoints at FBI headquarters in Washington, D.C., and made his way to the twelfth floor. His stomach tightened as he approached the conference room. This meeting could make or break everything.

Renfro, a man in his forties wearing a crisp suit and carrying an all-business demeanor, stood beside Barnes, who was forty-five with a vocal negative attitude that showed in every line of his face. Director Mitchell, fifty and impeccably dressed, sat behind a large mahogany desk, his grim expression unchanging as Sean entered.

Sean shook hands with the agents, then Mitchell.

"Sean Lugullo, Houston office," Sean said.

Mitchell stood, his expression remaining grim. "Nice to see you, Agent Lugullo. This is Renfro and Barnes. They're with the Secret Service."

Barnes barely waited for the introduction to finish. "You have something for us?"

Sean took a breath. "We've been investigating a terrorist cell from Syria who we believe killed Senator Richardson."

"What makes you say that?" Renfro asked, his tone skeptical.

"My sons play a war game online, and this cell is an opposing team."

Sean paused, knowing how ridiculous the next part would sound. "Evidence points to them as the assassins, and we believe they'll target the president next."

Renfro and Barnes focused on Sean. Barnes wore a smirk that made Sean's jaw tighten.

"Did you track them? Were they in Houston at the time?" Barnes asked.

"We suspect they used new technology in the game to teleport to where the senator was, shoot her, then leave the same way."

Renfro laughed and looked at Mitchell. "Is this a goddamn joke? I know they've been experimenting with teleportation — to an extent — but the last I heard, nothing works."

Sean kept his voice steady. "I know how this sounds, but it's no joke. They used this technology to teleport to my house, and they attempted to firebomb it."

"Is this about revenge?" Barnes leaned back in his chair, arms crossed.

"Not at all." Sean felt frustration building. He'd known this would be hard, but he hadn't expected outright mockery. "All right, listen, if you won't believe me, at least use a decoy."

"What?" Renfro said.

"A decoy. Use a double for the president. If nothing happens, no one needs to know, but if someone tries something, we're covered."

Director Mitchell stood, his chair scraping against the floor. The room went quiet. "I see nothing wrong with that. In fact, I think it's a good approach."

Mitchell turned to face Sean directly. "Agent Lugullo, if you're right about this, you'll be a hero, but if you're wrong, you'll be a laughing stock."

"I hope I'm wrong, sir," Sean said.

"Renfro, you and Barnes better get to the president and let him know."

Renfro's smirk disappeared, and he nodded curtly. "Yes, sir."

As the Secret Service agents left, Mitchell gestured for Sean to stay. "Sit down, Lugullo."

Sean sat.

Mitchell walked to the window, looking out over the city. "I've been in this job for twenty-three years. I've seen a lot of crazy things. But teleportation? That's new."

"I know how it sounds —"

"You keep saying that." Mitchell turned to face him. "But you witnessed it yourself. Is that correct?"

"Yes, sir. A member of my son's team teleported from his bedroom to my kitchen using the game's portal system."

"And this technology exists in a video game?"

"Yes, sir. We believe it's being tested through the game platform. Players don't realize they're part of the experiment."

Mitchell was quiet for a long moment. "If you're right, and this technology is operational, we're looking at a complete paradigm shift in how we approach security. No location would be secure."

"That's why we need to act now, sir. Before they realize we know."

"The funeral is in three days. That's not much time to prepare."

"It's enough, sir. We just need the decoy in place and agents positioned at key locations."

Mitchell nodded slowly. "All right. But if this goes sideways, it's your career on the line. Not mine."

"Understood, sir."

That afternoon, Barnes and Renfro stood beside the presidential limousine, waiting. President Hatcher, fifty-five with gray hair on the sides, walked toward them with his characteristic determined, confident stride. He waved to people as he approached the limo.

"Sir," Barnes said, his voice hesitant, "we think it may be better to use a decoy for the funeral."

President Hatcher stopped, his hand on the limo door. "A decoy? Richardson was my friend."

"I realize that, sir," Renfro said, "but the best thing you can do to honor her memory is stay alive to fight the cause she was so passionate about."

"And I can do that best by —"

Barnes interrupted, something he rarely did with the president.

"Sir, we believe her assassination was the act of a terrorist cell from Syria, and it's logical to assume you'll be a target as well."

President Hatcher's expression hardened. "If you're that concerned …"

Renfro stepped closer. "With all due respect, sir, I'm more worried about my job. If you get shot, or worse, killed, I'll be out of a job, and it's one I'm good at."

Hatcher laughed loudly, the tension breaking. "All right, Renfro. That convinced me. Tell me what to do."

Renfro pulled out his phone and began outlining the plan. "We'll use Agent Morrison as your double. He's your height, similar build, even some similar looks. With makeup and the right positioning, no one will know the difference from a distance."

"And where will I be?"

"In a secure location, watching via video feed."

Hatcher didn't like it — that much was clear from his expression. But he nodded. "Fine. But if this turns out to be nothing, someone's going to answer for wasting my time."

"Understood, sir," Barnes said.

As the president climbed into the limo, Renfro and Barnes exchanged glances. Barnes pulled out his phone and called Sean.

"Lugullo? It's Barnes. The president's on board with the decoy plan."

"Good," Sean said. "Now we need to make sure we're ready when they make their move."

"You really think they'll try something?"

"I know they will. The question is whether we'll be ready for them."

Barnes hung up and looked at Renfro. "You believe any of this teleportation stuff?"

Renfro shrugged. "It doesn't matter what I believe. What matters is keeping the president alive."

"Fair point."

They climbed into their own vehicle and followed the presidential motorcade. Behind them, unmarked FBI vehicles took up positions. The net was being cast.

Now they just had to wait and see what they caught.

Back at FBI headquarters, Sean sat at his desk reviewing the security plans for the funeral. Every detail had to be perfect. One mistake and the president's decoy could be dead. Or worse, they could miss their chance to catch the terrorists.

His phone buzzed. It was a text from Sorenson: *Tech guys analyzed the equipment from Al-Mansour's apartment. You're not going to believe what they found.*

Sean called him immediately. "What is it?"

"Quantum entanglement devices. Military-grade GPS systems. And something they're calling a 'spatial displacement module.' According to our experts, it's theoretical technology that shouldn't exist yet."

"But it does exist."

"Apparently. They're still trying to figure out how it works, but the preliminary analysis suggests it could create temporary wormholes between two GPS coordinates."

Sean leaned back in his chair. "Teleportation."

"That's the theory. And if Al-Mansour had this equipment, chances are the rest of his cell does too."

"Which means they can hit the president from anywhere."

"Exactly. I'm sending the full report to Mitchell now."

After Sorenson hung up, Sean stared at his computer screen. The pieces were falling into place. The technology was real. The threat was real. Now they just needed to stop it before someone else died.

His phone rang again. It was Joey.

"Dad, can we leave the house?"

"Not yet, son. A few more days."

"We've been cooped up here for two days. It would be great to get out for a little bit before we get to the last games."

"I'm working on it. Just stay put for now."

After he hung up, Sean called Mitchell. "Sir, I need permission to let my sons play in the tournament tomorrow night."

"Are you out of your mind?"

"No, sir. Think about it. If WolfDen *is* the terrorist cell, they'll have to show up for the game. It's the perfect opportunity to catch them."

Mitchell was quiet for a long moment. "That's using your kids as bait, Lugullo."

"Not really, sir. WolfDen can't do anything to them while they're inside the game. Besides, they're already targets. At least this way, we'd know where WolfDen is."

"Let me think about it. I'll call you back."

Sean hung up and waited. The clock on his wall ticked loudly in the silence. Everything was converging — the funeral, the tournament, and the investigation. In three days, it would all come to a head.

Chapter Forty
THE FUNERAL

Two nights later, Sean sat at the kitchen table drinking a beer when Tony walked in. The house felt quiet despite the FBI agents stationed outside. Too quiet.

"How'd it go in D.C.?" Tony asked, grabbing an energy drink from the fridge.

Sean set his beer down. "They didn't believe anything I said. Despite that, I think I convinced them to at least use a decoy which is better than nothing."

"I hope it's someone without kids," Tony said, his voice flat.

Sean looked up at his son. The kid had killed a man a few nights ago and now he was talking about presidential security like it was normal conversation. *When did everything get so surreal?*

"You really think so?"

Tony nodded, a somber look on his face. "I'd bet money on it."

"How do you think they'll do it?"

Tony pulled out a chair and sat down across from his father. "I haven't seen the layout, but they'll probably wait until things are calm, like when he's giving a speech, then they'll teleport in, attack, and be back out before anyone notices." He paused. "I've seen them play a lot of games, and I know their strategy."

Sean took a sip of his beer and stared at his son. *Seventeen years old and he's analyzing terrorist tactics.* "You really think so?"

"I know so." Tony's voice was certain. "They're aggressive but disciplined. They don't take unnecessary risks. They'll hit hard, hit fast, and disappear before anyone can react."

"And if the Secret Service is ready for them?"

"Then they'll adapt. But Dad, they're not expecting teleportation. Even though you told them, they won't prepare for it. That's Wolf-Den's advantage."

Sean thought about the meeting in D.C., and the skepticism on Barnes and Renfro's faces. "I tried to tell them."

"I know you did." Tony stood up. "You did everything you could. The rest is up to them."

After Tony left, Sean sat alone in the kitchen, finishing his beer. Tomorrow was the funeral. He hoped Tony was wrong. But he knew he wasn't.

On the day of Senator Richardson's funeral, lines of cars stretched for half a mile, waiting to enter St. Elizabeth's Cemetery. There was only one road in and out, and it was heavily guarded.

Secret Service agents and police officers manned the entrance gate, checking IDs, searching vehicles, running background checks on every attendee. More agents stood at checkpoints along the winding cemetery road. When the last car entered, the Secret Service closed the gate and stationed armed guards there.

The morning was cold and gray, fitting for a funeral. Clouds hung low over the cemetery, threatening rain.

Soon, the presidential motorcade arrived, driving slowly. Black SUVs flanked the main vehicle on all sides. The motorcade stopped at the gate and waited while the Secret Service opened it for them.

Barnes rode in the lead vehicle, constantly scanning the perimeter. He spoke into his comm. "Eagle is approaching the site. All units, report status."

One by one, the teams checked in. Snipers were positioned on the nearby hills, and agents spread throughout the cemetery. Bomb-sniffing dogs had swept the area twice. Everything was secure.

The motorcade parked close to the gravesite, and the president's decoy — Agent Morrison — stepped out. He wore a dark suit, sunglasses, and a thick scarf around his neck to help conceal his features. From a distance, he was a perfect match.

Barnes walked beside him. "Don't worry, sir. The podium is protected with plexiglass that has withstood a barrage of fifty-caliber shots. You're safe."

The decoy nodded but said nothing. He'd been briefed extensively. Walk like the president. Wave like him. Speak with his cadence and inflection. Be him in every way.

He walked to the podium, waving to the crowd of mourners gathered around Senator Richardson's grave. Several hundred people had come to pay their respects. Senators, congressmen, foreign dignitaries, family members. All of them waiting to hear the president speak.

The decoy placed his hands on the podium and began. "This is one of the saddest days of my life. Senator Richardson was not only a professional colleague but a friend. We had similar views on many subjects and were in a position to end this rash of international terrorism."

His voice carried across the cemetery through strategically placed speakers. The crowd listened in respectful silence.

Near the back of the cemetery, behind a thick tree trunk, Sandof appeared. One moment the space was empty, the next he was there — materialized out of nothing with a soft shimmer of displaced air. In his hands, he carried a rocket launcher.

Twenty yards away, behind an ornate marble mausoleum, Rizwan appeared the same way. He carried a rifle with a high-powered scope.

None of the Secret Service agents saw them materialize. They were watching the crowd, the perimeter, the known entry points. Not the empty spaces that suddenly weren't empty anymore.

The decoy took a sip of water and continued. "I see this as a testament that Senator Richardson was having a strong effect on the terrorists and that they were growing nervous — afraid of her influence."

Sandof peeked out from the side of the tree. He adjusted the launcher on his shoulder, checking the sight line. The podium was two hundred yards away. An easy shot.

He waited until the Secret Service agents near the podium shifted positions, creating a clear line of fire. Then he pressed the button.

The missile launched forward with a whoosh of displaced air. It streaked across the cemetery on a direct path toward the podium. The flight time was less than two seconds.

Before the decoy could get another sentence out, the missile hit the bottom half of the podium and exploded.

The blast was deafening. The plexiglass shattered into a thousand pieces. The decoy was thrown backward, his body torn apart by shrapnel and concussive force. Two Secret Service agents standing nearby were killed instantly.

Chaos erupted. People screamed and ran. Secret Service agents drew their weapons, searching for the shooter. Barnes yelled into his comm, "Shots fired! Shots fired! Eagle is down!"

But even as he said it, he was running toward the tree where Sandof had been. He got there in fifteen seconds.

The space was empty.

"Suspect fled!" Barnes shouted. "Heading —" He stopped. There were no footprints in the soft grass. No sign anyone had been there at all.

Across the cemetery, Renfro reached the mausoleum where Rizwan had been. Same thing. Empty. No trace.

"How the fuck did this happen?" Barnes said, staring at the empty ground.

Renfro joined him, breathing hard. "Maybe we should have listened to Lugullo."

Barnes pulled out his phone and called Sean. His hands were shaking. "They did it. Just like you said. Teleported in, fired, and disappeared."

"Casualties?" Sean asked, his voice tight.

"Three dead. Morrison and two other agents. The real president is secure."

"Any sign of the shooters?"

"They're gone. No footprints, no shell casings, nothing. It's like they were never here."

Sean closed his eyes. He'd warned them. And three people were still dead.

"I'm coming to D.C.," Sean said. "We need to end this before they kill anyone else."

"Agreed, Lugullo? But how do we fight an enemy that can appear and disappear at will?"

"We find where they're coming from. And we shut it down."

After Barnes hung up, he looked at Renfro. The other agent's face was pale.

"Teleportation," Renfro said quietly. "It's real."

"Yeah. It is."

They walked back toward the blast site. Emergency personnel were already there, tending to the wounded, covering the dead. The senator's funeral had become a massacre.

At the house, Sean hung up the phone and sat down heavily. Joey, Tony, Brie, Pete, and Ritchie were gathered in the living room, watching the news coverage.

"Dad?" Joey said. "What happened?"

"They killed the decoy. Just like Tony predicted."

Tony's face went pale. "I was hoping I was wrong."

"You weren't." Sean looked at each of them. "The final game is tomorrow night. I got approval from Mitchell. You're playing."

"What?" Missy said from the doorway. "Absolutely not. These people are killers."

"They can't kill them inside the game. They'll be safe while they're playing."

"Are you trying to get them killed?" Missy asked.

Sean met her eyes. "I already told you that won't happen. I promise, Missy. I would never let anything happen to them."

She stared at him for a long moment, then turned and walked away. Sean heard the bedroom door slam.

He looked back at the kids. "Tomorrow night. The tournament venue. We end this."

Joey nodded. "We're ready."

"I hope so," Sean said. "Because if we're not, more people are going to die."

Chapter Forty-One
THE LAST PRACTICE

That night, Tony entered Joey's bedroom and saw Pete sitting on the sofa. Joey and Brie were on beanbag chairs on the floor. An extra beanbag sat open for Tony. He laughed as he settled into it.

"What's the plan?" Brie asked.

"Same as last time," Joey said. "We go to the shack and wait for them to show."

"I think we should switch," Tony said. "They're onto us by now."

"Not after one time. No way."

"I'm telling you, they've been reactive with their strategy every time. We should switch."

Pete shook his head. "I disagree. This worked last time, so let's go for it."

"Looks like you're outvoted," Joey said.

"Not so fast." Brie sat up straighter. "I'm with Tony. He seems to know what they'll do next, almost like he knows their plan."

Joey sighed. "Okay, Tony's plan it is. This is the last practice, so get it right."

They logged in. The screen flashed: Piney Woods — Night.

Brie led the team forward, all of them crawling on their stomachs through the dense forest undergrowth.

"Stay below the foliage near the edge," she whispered through the comm. "We can't let them see us."

She moved forward and then headed east, passing the shack and other structures. Once they were clear, she headed north until she reached a spot that offered good protection behind large boulders surrounded by small, bushy ferns.

The ferns provided great cover and allowed good visibility of the shack, but they made a lot of noise when someone crawled through them. Brie carefully parted the leaves and peeked through. No one was near the shack.

"Stay put," she said. "And be quiet."

Joey and Pete moved into position behind her.

"Where's Tony?" Brie asked.

"He was with us a minute ago," Joey said.

Tony lay flat on the ground thirty feet behind them. "I'm behind you, dickhead. Somebody's gotta cover your ass."

"Stay behind us and keep watch," Brie said.

"I don't need to keep watch. You're making so much noise, it's easier to follow the sound."

Tall weeds moved to the south of Joey, as if blowing in a breeze. Tony heard the noise, then spotted the movement.

"I've got movement fifty yards south and moving west," he said.

"I'm tracking him," Brie said. "Everybody get a bead on him, and we'll fire at once."

Tony responded quickly. "No shooting. Let me handle it. Repeat. No shooting."

He crawled forward at a snail's pace, taking care not to rustle leaves or stir branches or weeds. The forest floor was a minefield of sound — every stick, every dry leaf could give him away. He controlled his breathing, moving with the patience of a hunter.

As he got closer to the enemy, he drew his knife, a long serrated blade with a curved tip. The weapon gleamed dully in the moonlight filtering through the trees.

He got within three feet of the soldier, then rushed him and slit his throat in one smooth motion. The enemy's character dissolved into pixels.

"This is our scenario, y'all," Tony said. "We own it. So use it to our advantage. No guns unless absolutely necessary."

Brie settled in behind a fallen tree and used a branch to cover herself. She heard the rustle of leaves and slid closer to the tree, careful not to make noise.

Rizwan advanced slowly, silently making his way through the forest. He stepped over the fallen tree that Brie was hiding under, lifted his rifle, and aimed at Pete, who was twenty yards ahead.

He was about to pull the trigger when Brie yanked his legs out from under him. He fell face-first to the ground, and she quickly jammed her knife into his hamstring, then crawled up and stabbed the back of his neck repeatedly. The character went limp.

"Stay put and wait for them to come to us," Brie said. "Don't stick your head out or take any chances. Wait until you have a clear shot at them."

"I'll climb the tree to get a better view," Tony said.

Joey poked his head out and looked for signs of the enemy. A shot hit the boulder close to his head, sending virtual rock fragments flying. He ducked behind it and reloaded his rifle.

"Goddamn, he almost got me," Joey said.

"Stay put until I tell you. Got it?" Brie's voice was firm.

"Got it."

Tony sat in his perch high in the tree and scanned the area. The elevated position gave him a clear view of the battlefield. He spied an enemy west of them, barely visible and closing in on Joey. Tony judged the distance with his laser rangefinder, then calculated the crosswind by watching the movement of leaves.

He closed his eyes and concentrated, visualizing the shot. Then he aimed and fired, hitting the enemy in the chest. He shot again and hit the gut, taking him out.

"Goddamn, Tony. Damn good shooting," Joey said.

"Only one to go," Brie said.

She crept south, followed by Joey and Pete. They moved in single file, weapons ready.

"You're headed the wrong way," Tony said from his perch. "He'll come in from the west."

"No way," Joey said.

Tony adjusted his position and scanned the area. "Suit yourself."

Joey held up his fist, signaling a halt. Then he turned. "Get behind the rocks ahead."

The last of the WolfDen team advanced from the west, keeping low so he wasn't seen. He moved with the skill of someone who'd done this hundreds of times.

Tony spied him and reported his location. "Enemy advancing from the west, fifty or sixty yards ahead."

Brie signaled a stop, and they took cover while watching for signs of advancement. Soon, Brie noticed the grass moving in an unnatural pattern, against the wind.

"He's twenty yards ahead and advancing slowly," she whispered. "Be prepared."

Joey, Pete, and Brie sat motionless. The forest around them was silent except for the distant sound of wind through the trees. Soon, they saw the grass ahead of them stirring again.

They took aim, fingers on triggers. But a shot rang out from Tony's position, dropping the last of the WolfDen team.

Joey rushed forward and finished the job with three final shots to make sure. He returned to Pete and Brie and high-fived them both.

"That makes it three to two in the practice sessions," Joey said. "We're ready."

Brie shook her head, a look of admiration on her face. "I've never seen a better sniper than Tony. And he seems to know what they'll do next. It's scary."

"That's what makes him good," Pete said.

Tony climbed down from his perch and joined them. "They're predictable. That's their weakness. They've been using the same strategies for months because they've been winning. They don't think they need to change."

"But we changed," Joey said.

"Exactly. And tomorrow night, that's going to make all the difference."

Back in the house, they logged out of the game. The room was quiet for a moment as they processed what had just happened.

"That was our best run yet," Pete said.

"Because we adapted," Tony said. "WolfDen's good, but they're rigid. They stick to what works. We're learning to improvise."

Brie stood and stretched. "So tomorrow's the real thing."

"Plus we catch some terrorists," Ritchie added from the corner. "Don't forget that part."

Joey looked at each of them. "Everyone get some rest tonight. Tomorrow's going to be intense."

After the others left, Tony lingered by the door. "You nervous?"

"About the game or the terrorists?" Joey asked.

"Both."

"Yeah. I'm nervous."

"Good," Tony said. "That means you're taking it seriously."

"It's hard not to when people are trying to kill us."

Tony smiled grimly. "Fair point. But don't worry, Joey. We're going to win tomorrow. I know it."

"How can you be so sure?"

"Because there's no other option."

After Tony left, Joey lay on his bed staring at the ceiling.

Outside his window, FBI agents patrolled the perimeter. Somewhere out there, WolfDen was preparing too. Planning their next move. Getting ready for the final game.

Chapter Forty-Two
YOU'LL HAVE TO MISS A GAME

That night in Joey's bedroom, the team was ecstatic, laughing and high-fiving each other after their practice victory.

"Only one more win and we're the champs," Joey said, grinning.

Brie's expression sobered. "Let's not forget their real goal—to kill the president. And it's up to us to stop them."

"Fuck the president," Pete said. "He doesn't care about us."

"He's still the president," Tony said quietly.

The celebration died down. What they were actually involved in settled over the room like a heavy blanket. This wasn't just about a tournament anymore. People were dying.

Brie stood and grabbed her jacket. "I should head back to my room. It's a big day tomorrow."

After everyone left, Joey sat alone, the glow of his monitor the only light. Tomorrow was the final game. Tomorrow they'd face WolfDen for real.

The next morning, Tony went to the kitchen and sat next to his father. Sean was hunched over his laptop, the coffee growing cold beside him.

"What's up, Dad?"

Sean looked up, his face drawn and tired. "Getting ready for a big meeting with the Secret Service."

"What are they screwing up now?"

"The decoy was killed at Senator Richardson's funeral."

Tony nodded slowly. "That means the president will be killed at the decoy's funeral."

"There's no way that will happen," Sean said firmly.

Tony laughed sarcastically. "Leave it up to them and the president is as good as dead."

"Come on, Tony. The Secret Service is the best in the world."

"Apparently not."

Sean nodded and looked at his son for a long moment. Tony had grown up so much in the past few days. The kid who'd shot a terrorist with a pellet gun. The gamer who understood tactics better than trained agents. When had his teenage son become someone he needed to consult on national security?

"I need to go to bed," Sean finally said, closing his laptop. "I've got an early flight to D.C. tomorrow."

But sleep didn't come easily. Sean lay awake thinking about the funeral, the attack, the three dead agents. If Tony was right and they tried again at the decoy's funeral, how many more would die?

Around midnight, Sean gave up on sleep. He walked down the hallway, stopping at Joey's door. Light showed under the crack.

Sean flicked the light and sat on the sofa beside Joey, who looked up from his phone, surprised.

"You never come in here, Dad."

Sean exhaled and pursed his lips. "I need to ask you something." He paused. "We think the terrorists plan to assassinate the president, and your brother doesn't think the Secret Service can stop them."

Joey chuckled, shaking his head. "I'd listen to him."

"You really think so?"

Joey leaned back, a worried look crossing his face. "The last game we played, all of us were sure WolfDen would attack from the south. I even thought I saw movement. But Tony insisted they'd come from the west." He paused. "He was so sure, he stayed put even when we all moved south." Another pause. "And he was right. Not only that, but he made two kill shots that real snipers would envy."

Joey met his father's gaze, his voice steady. "So, yeah. I'd listen to him."

Sean nodded slowly, absorbing every word. His younger son — the one who could barely keep his room clean, who lacked social skills, and who drove his mother crazy — had instincts that professional agents lacked.

"Thanks," Sean said, standing up.

"Dad?" Joey called as Sean reached the door. "Bring him back safe, okay? We need him for the final game."

"I will. I promise."

Sean headed to Tony's room. Tony was almost asleep when Sean opened the door.

"You still awake?" Sean asked.

Tony pulled his covers off and looked at his dad. "Yeah, what's up?"

"Do you really think you can help the Secret Service protect him?"

"I know I can."

Sean studied his son's face. There was no hesitation, no doubt. Just certainty. "Pack a bag. We're flying to D.C. in the morning."

"What time?"

"Six AM. And Tony?" Sean paused. "This is serious. Lives depend on getting this right."

"I know, Dad. That's why I'm going."

After Sean left, Tony lay back down, but sleep was impossible now. He was going to D.C. to advise the Secret Service.

It was insane. But he knew WolfDen's tactics better than anyone. He'd studied them for months, watched hundreds of hours of gameplay, learned how they thought. If anyone could predict their next move, it was him. He just hoped the Secret Service would actually listen.

. . .

The next morning, Tony re-entered Joey's bedroom with a frown covering his face. Pete and Brie were already there, getting ready for practice.

"We're gonna have to get Ritchie for the next game," Tony said. "I have to help Dad."

"With what?" Joey asked.

"The Secret Service wants to ask questions about WolfDen, in case they go after the president."

"This sucks." Joey stood up, agitated. "We can't win with Ritchie, and besides, who gives a shit about the president?"

He sucked hard on a dry cigarette, not even bothering to light it.

"Enough Joey!" Tony's voice was sharp. "I told Dad I'd do it, so I'm going with him And we leave in half an hour."

Joey stared at his brother. He wanted to argue that the tournament was more important, but he knew it wasn't true. People were dying. The president could be next. And if Tony could help stop it, then he had to go.

"Fine," Joey said quietly. He grabbed his phone. "That means we need to get Ritchie lined up. He'll need practice before the next game."

Joey listened as the phone rang. Once. Twice. Three times. Finally, Ritchie picked up.

"Ritchie, it's Joey. Got a minute?"

"Go on," Ritchie's voice came through, groggy with sleep.

"We need you today. It's the final game and we're even, so we really need this win."

"Who's not going to make it?"

"Tony won't be here. He's got to advise the FBI on something."

"Son of a bitch!" Ritchie laughed. "He's in the big-time, huh?"

Joey managed a laugh. "I don't know about the big time, but he'll be busy, so we need you."

"Count me in. I'll be over in a few."

Joey hung up and looked at Tony. "You really think you can help them?"

"Yeah. I do."

"Then go. We'll manage without you for one game."

Tony nodded. "Thanks, Joey. And listen — don't go easy on WolfDen just because I'm not there. You beat them in practice. You can beat them for real."

"We'll try."

After Tony left to pack, Joey sat back down on the couch. Brie moved closer.

"You okay?" she asked.

"No. We're playing the final game without our best sniper, against a team of actual terrorists." He looked at her. "How is any of this okay?"

"It's not," Brie said. "But we do it anyway."

Pete spoke up from his beanbag. "So who's calling this game? You or Ritchie?"

"Me," Joey said. "Ritchie's good, but he's not a leader. I'll call the shots. You and Brie just need to trust me."

"We always have," Brie said.

Joey pulled out his phone and started texting his father: *Good luck in D.C. Bring Tony home safe.*

The response came a minute later: *Will do. Win that tournament.*

Joey smiled despite everything. His father believed in them. Tony believed in them. Now they just had to believe in themselves.

"All right," Joey said, standing up. "Ritchie will be here in an hour. Let's run through strategies until then. We've got one shot at this, and we're not going to blow it."

Chapter Forty-Three
A VISIT TO D.C.

Sean entered the FBI building in Washington D.C. and stood in line for security screening. Tony trailed him by a few steps, looking around at the imposing architecture and the serious-faced agents moving through the lobby.

The building felt different than the Houston office. It was bigger, and it seemed more important. It was definitely more intimidating.

They placed their phones and keys in plastic bins, walked through the metal detector, and collected their belongings on the other side. A guard checked Sean's credentials and waved them through.

They took the elevator to the twenty-fifth floor. The elevator was silent except for the soft ding as they passed each floor. Tony stood rigid, his hands clasped in front of him.

When they got off, Sean whispered to Tony as they went down the hallway. "I want you to keep quiet unless spoken to. If they ask you a question, answer, but if not —"

"I know how it works, Dad. It's like the principal's office."

Sean looked questioningly at Tony but remained silent.

As they neared the end of the hall, Sean tapped Tony's arm and headed to Director Mitchell' office. The door was open, revealing a large conference room with a long table.

"Take a seat, son," Sean said.

Sitting in chairs opposite them were Barnes and Renfro, the Secret Service men Sean had met before. They nodded when Sean sat. Their expressions were neutral but wary. They weren't happy about being here, that much was clear.

Tony took the seat next to his father, his posture straight, his face serious. He looked older than seventeen in that moment.

Director Mitchell entered a few seconds later, carrying a file folder and a cup of coffee. "Forgive me for being late, gentlemen."

"In many countries, they view lateness as a sign of disrespect," Tony said.

Sean kicked Tony's leg under the table and glared at him. What the hell was the kid thinking?

"Excuse me, sir, he —"

Director Mitchell smiled, holding up a hand. "It's fine, Sean. Your son is right. Tardiness is frowned upon in many countries — as it should be."

He bowed slightly to Tony, a gesture of respect that surprised Sean. "Kudos to your knowledge of foreign customs." He paused. "Where did you learn that?"

Tony looked to his father, then back to the director. "On YouTube, sir."

Director Mitchell laughed, a genuine sound that filled the room. "Son of a bitch, I guess I need to stop scolding my kids for watching YouTube." He set his coffee down and took his seat at the head of the table. "Let's cut to the chase, young man. Why do you think you can help us?"

Tony looked around at the other men in the room. Barnes and Renfro were watching him with skeptical expressions. His father looked nervous. Director Mitchell looked curious.

Barnes put his elbows on his knees and leaned forward. "Tony, we don't know if we need help, but we'd like to hear what you have to say." He paused. "This concerns the president's life."

"I understand, sir." Tony's voice was steady. "All I can say is that if you approach this the way you do everything else, the president will be as dead as the ones on the dollar bills."

Renfro sat up straight, his face reddening. "Wait a damn minute, boy. I've been protecting presidents half my life, and my record is untarnished, so don't try to tell me —"

"The decoy is dead," Tony said, looking directly at Renfro.

The room went silent. Renfro's mouth closed. The simple statement hung in the air like an accusation.

Sean watched the exchange, torn between pride in his son's courage and fear that Tony had just made powerful enemies. But Tony was right. The decoy had died under their protection. That was an undeniable fact.

Director Mitchell leaned close to Barnes and whispered, "Barnes, you need to let him scour the funeral grounds and see what he suggests."

"But, sir —"

"It will be your ass if something happens and you didn't listen," Mitchell said, his voice quiet but firm.

Barnes looked at Renfro, who shrugged. The anger had left his face, replaced by resignation. "I agree with the director. Does no harm to take him with us."

Sean stared and shook his head. "I don't want him there for anything but advice. I won't put his life at risk."

"Take it easy, Lugullo," Barnes said. "We're not suggesting he guard the president. We're simply asking that he visit the funeral site and suggest defensive tactics based on his knowledge of the terrorist group."

Tony reached over and tapped his father's arm. "I'll go."

Sean looked at his son. Tony's expression was determined, unflinching. *When had he gotten so brave? Or maybe he'd always been brave and I didn't notice.*

"Sean," Director Mitchell said, "I suggest you accompany your son to the site, and when you're ready to leave, I'll have a plane ready."

Mitchell walked over to Tony and patted him on the back. "You're an honorable and brave young man, Tony."

Tony stood and shook the director's hand. "Thank you, sir. I just want to help."

As they left the office, Barnes and Renfro followed them into the hallway. Barnes pulled Sean aside while Renfro stood with Tony.

"Your kid's got guts," Barnes said quietly. "But Lugullo, if he's wrong about this —"

"He's not wrong," Sean said. "I've watched him play against this team for months. He knows their tactics better than anyone."

"He's seventeen years old."

"Age doesn't matter when traditional security measures don't apply. You need someone who thinks like them, and who understands how they operate."

Barnes nodded slowly. "All right. We'll listen to what he has to say. But if I think he's putting the president at risk with bad advice —"

"Then you ignore him. But at least hear him out."

"Fair enough."

They regrouped in the hallway. Renfro was actually smiling at something Tony had said. The ice was breaking, slowly.

"We've got a car waiting," Renfro said. "We'll head to the cemetery so Tony can look around."

"Sounds good," Sean said.

As they walked to the elevator, Tony fell into step beside his father. "Thanks for believing in me, Dad."

"Always, son. Just don't make me regret it."

Tony smiled. "I'll try not to."

During the car ride, Tony seemed calm, almost serene. He scrolled through his phone, reviewing footage of WolfDen's gameplay, and analyzing their strategies.

"You nervous?" Sean asked quietly.

"Terrified," Tony admitted. "But it's like before a big game. The nerves go away once you start playing."

"This isn't a game."

"I know, Dad. But the tactics are the same. WolfDen operates on predictable patterns. They're good, but they're not creative. They stick to what works."

"And what works for them?"

"Hit hard, hit fast, disappear. They don't do prolonged engagements. They strike when their target is most vulnerable, then they're gone before anyone can react."

Barnes, who'd been listening from the front seat, turned around. "So when do you think they'll strike at the funeral?"

"During the eulogy," Tony said without hesitation. "Maximum emotional impact. Everyone's focused on the speaker, guards are stationary, and there's a clear line of sight to the podium."

"We'll have the podium shielded," Renfro said.

"That won't matter if they teleport next to it. Or behind it. Or above it."

The car went quiet again.

"So what do we do?" Barnes asked.

"We'll talk about it at the site," Tony said. "I need to see the layout first."

Sean looked at his son with a mixture of pride and fear. Tony sounded so sure and confident. But if he was wrong and his advice failed, people would die. And Tony would have to live with that for the rest of his life.

The car pulled to a stop, and as they got out, Sean's phone buzzed. It was a text from Joey: *How's it going?*

Sean typed back: *Good. Tony's impressing everyone.*

Of course he is. He's a Lugullo.

Sean smiled and put his phone away. Whatever happened next, at least his sons had confidence in each other. He just hoped it was enough.

Tony carried a game system under his arm, and he had his phone in the other hand.

As they walk toward the site where the president would be, Sean patted Tony's back. "I know missing the next game puts you in a bind, but we'll get back as soon as we can."

"I'm just hoping we get back for game seven. And don't let me forget to take this system back with us."

"Who knows, maybe they'll win without you."

Tony chuckled and then broke into a full laugh.

Chapter Forty-Four
DESERT SANDS

Joey adjusted the settings on his remote to reflect his desert camouflage while instructing the others.

"Pete, I know you've played the desert scenario before, but for Brie and Ritchie, listen up."

Joey looked at each of them to make sure they were paying attention. "You won't have any place to hide except for an occasional oasis, and even then it's only a few trees."

He pulled up a map of the Desert Sands scenario on his tablet. "In the desert, you need to rely on your uniforms to camouflage you or, if you're lucky, you might hide behind a dune or lie still in a pocket of sand." He paused. "Either way, nothing will last long, so be ready to take a shot, and it needs to be on target because if you shoot and miss, they'll return fire immediately."

"Got it," Brie said.

"I'm ready," Ritchie added, though his voice betrayed some nervousness.

Joey studied Ritchie's face. He was trying hard, but he wasn't Tony. Regardless, they had to work with what they had.

"One more thing," Joey said. "Without Tony calling positions from a sniper perch, we're going to have to be more careful about communication. Call out everything you see. Don't assume someone else spotted it."

They all nodded and logged into the game.

∼

The GhostWalkers materialized in an oasis with a small pond and half a dozen palm trees. A knee-high wall built from bricks and stones surrounded the oasis so it wasn't overrun with windblown sand.

The heat hit them immediately, even through the game's interface. The suits made everything feel real.

Joey bent down and filled his canteen from the pond. The water looked cool and inviting, though he knew it was just pixels. "And don't forget, this is like all the other scenarios. Things will feel real. You'll get hot as hell, the wind will blow sand in your face, and more. So fill your canteens and drink sparingly. Water is like gold here."

The others filled their canteens while Joey stood guard. He scanned the horizon in all directions but there was nothing but sand and heat shimmer as far as he could see.

Pete and Ritchie pulled out their binoculars and peered in all directions as well.

"I've got nothing. I mean *nothing*," Pete said.

"Same here," Ritchie added. "If they're in range, they're invisible."

"Look again," Joey said. "The camouflage can make a person appear invisible, and WolfDen is used to it."

Brie removed a pair of binoculars from a pocket on her suit, wiped the lenses clean, and handed them to Ritchie. "Use these binoculars. They're better."

Ritchie reluctantly let his binoculars dangle on his neck strap and grabbed the pair Brie handed him. He searched the barren desert from the west and then all the way around. The improved optics made a significant difference. He could see details he'd missed before.

When he neared the south, he dropped to his knees. "Get down. They're advancing from the south."

Everyone dropped to their knees and positioned themselves. Joey's heart rate picked up.

"I'll keep watch to the west," Brie said. "Y'all look north and east."

"The east is blocked by the cliffs of Mount Sharaga," Joey said. "No need to look."

"Still advancing, but slowly," Ritchie said.

"Keep below the wall and stay alert," Brie said. "I'll stay here."

"Sounds good," Joey said.

Joey, Ritchie, and Pete hunkered down behind the southern wall and continued watching the WolfDen team advance. The enemy moved with practiced efficiency, keeping low, using every bit of cover the desert provided. These guys were good. Really good.

Ritchie peered through his binoculars, then adjusted them and looked again. "They're still moving slowly, but I only see two of them."

"Stay alert," Joey said. That meant two were hidden somewhere. He scanned the area more carefully, looking for any shimmer in the air.

Brie got her binoculars back from Ritchie and carefully scanned, going from north to west, ignoring the eastern front. Meanwhile, Joey scanned the south.

"The one on the west side is moving, Ritchie. Can you get him?"

"Watch me."

Ritchie took aim and fired twice. Both shots kicked up sand several feet from the target. He'd led too much, compensating for movement that wasn't there.

"Goddamnit," Pete said. "Tony would have gotten him."

Ritchie snapped back at Pete. "Tony's not here, asshole. Can you do better?"

"I know I couldn't have made the shot," Joey said, trying to defuse the tension. "Let's see if Brie can." He keyed his comm. "Hey, Brie. We need you over here."

Brie crossed the oasis in a crouch and got to the southern wall next to Joey. "What's up?"

Joey pointed to the WolfDen members south of them. "Watch the one on the west side. When he moves, take him out."

Brie placed her rifle on the wall and scoped in the enemy. She waited, her breathing steady and her finger resting lightly on the trigger. When he moved, she fired. Her shot was a direct hit. The enemy soldier dropped.

"Three to go," Brie said.

She turned to Joey and was about to say something when a shot hit her in the back. Seconds later, another shot hit. Brie's character crumpled.

"Damn it," Brie said in the real world, pulling off her headset.

Joey and Ritchie scrambled to the north wall. Pete crawled to safety behind a large palm tree, but he was exposed on one side.

"Pete, get your ass over here," Ritchie said. "You're too exposed."

"Let me worry about —"

A single shot hit him in the leg. When he reached to pull his leg in, another shot took him in the chest, removing him from the game.

In the house, Pete threw his controller down. "This is bullshit."

"Shit, Joey, we're two down," Ritchie said through the comm. "What are we gonna do?"

"We're gonna kick their ass." Joey forced confidence into his voice even though his mind was racing. They were outnumbered now, two against three. Not good odds. "See that small cluster of trees? If we make it there, it'll give us cover from three sides, and we can protect ourselves."

"I'll lay down cover while you scoot over there," Ritchie said. "When you're secure, you lay down cover for me."

Ritchie peered over the top of the wall and waited until he spotted movement. He fired, and the man stumbled. Ritchie fired again, hitting him in the chest. The enemy went down.

Two against two now. Better odds.

Joey dove for the cover of the trees, rolling as he landed and coming up behind the thickest trunk. He poked his head out and laid down covering fire for Ritchie, who ran for cover.

Cyrus crawled to the top of a dune and dug in until he was almost impossible to see. Only the top of his head and his rifle scope were visible above the sand. He scoped the oasis carefully. On the third inspection, he saw Ritchie's leg sticking out from a cluster of trees. He aimed and fired, hitting Ritchie just above the knee.

Ritchie howled in pain and pulled his leg back. "Goddamn. I'm hit. My leg."

"Can you walk?" Joey asked.

"Hell no. I can't even crawl."

Joey grabbed hold of Ritchie and pulled him deeper into the cluster of trees to give him better cover. Virtual blood stained the sand where Ritchie had been lying.

"Damn, this hurts," Ritchie said. The game's pain feedback wasn't pleasant. "What are we gonna do? I can't take this long."

"We're gonna stay put and out of sight," Joey said, thinking fast. "They need water, which means they'll have to come here soon." He paused. "When they do, we'll be waiting."

"Son of a bitch."

"Good God, stop moaning or they'll hear us. Just lie back and try to rest. I'll take first watch."

Joey settled in behind a tree trunk and scanned the desert. The sun was setting in the game, painting the sand in shades of orange and red. Beautiful, if it weren't for the two killers out there waiting for them.

Hours passed in the game. The desert night fell, bringing cold instead of heat. Joey shivered despite himself. The temperature simulation in these suits was impressive and uncomfortable in equal measure.

He reached over and shook Ritchie. "Your watch. Get up."

Ritchie groaned and mumbled as he crawled to the outer edge of the trees. "You see any activity?"

Joey shook his head. "Nothing. But make sure to use the night-vision goggles. It's almost impossible to see them."

Ritchie activated his night vision and scanned the areas north and west of the oasis. Everything showed up in shades of green. He saw nothing but sand and the occasional desert animal. He inched forward to get a better look, but when he did, he exposed the right side of his chest.

Cyrus, who'd been waiting for exactly this kind of mistake, took the shot. The bullet hit Ritchie in the chest, knocking him out of the game.

In the house, Ritchie pulled off his headset and swore.

Joey was alone now. One against two.

Ritchie's cry of pain in the game had roused Joey's character. He grabbed his gun and looked out, just in time to see Cyrus heading for cover behind a dune. Joey fired twice, hitting Cyrus in the back both times. The terrorist leader went down.

"Wish you were here to see this, Tony," Joey muttered. "We're gonna kick their —"

A shot rang out from the south as Rizwan fired. The bullet hit the tree close to Joey's head, sending bark fragments flying. Joey felt the impact through the suit's feedback system.

He spun and fired several times, his shots wild but one lucky. One bullet hit Rizwan in the left leg. The enemy soldier fell, then scrambled to his feet and limped off to the east. As he moved, he took aim and fired multiple times at Joey. Two bullets caught Joey in the chest, one in the leg.

Joey felt his character's health dropping. Red warnings flashing. He was dying. But he still had enough left for one shot.

He aimed carefully, leading Rizwan's limping movement, and fired.

The bullet hit Rizwan in the back of the head. Kill shot.

But Joey's character collapsed at the same moment, succumbing to his wounds.

The screen flashed: DRAW.

Back in the house, Joey pulled off his headset and threw it on the couch. "Damn it."

"That was close," Pete said.

"Close doesn't win tournaments," Joey said. "We needed that practice win. Now we're tied going into the final game."

Brie picked up her headset. "We need Tony back. I'm good, but I'm not sniper good like him."

"He'll be back tomorrow. Dad promised."

"And if he's not?" Ritchie asked.

Joey met his eyes. "Then we play anyway. We didn't come this far to give up now."

He pulled out his phone and texted Tony: *How's D.C.? We need you back tomorrow.*

The response came a minute later: *Working on it. Don't worry. I'll be there. How'd the game go?*

It was a draw. Not bad for Desert Sands.

Joey hoped that what Tony said was true, because without Tony, their chances of beating WolfDen in the final game had just gotten a lot worse.

"All right," Joey said, standing up. "Everyone get some rest. Tomorrow's the big day. The final game. Winner takes all."

After the others left to get sleep, Joey sat alone in the room. He stared at the black screen of his monitor, thinking about the game they'd just played. They'd lost Brie early because they hadn't been watching their backs. Pete had gotten too exposed. Ritchie had made a rookie mistake on watch.

Tony wouldn't have made those mistakes. Tony would have called out WolfDen's position before they could shoot Brie. Tony would have kept Pete covered. Tony would have stayed alert on watch.

But Tony wasn't here. And Joey was going to have to figure out how to win without him because he might not be there tomorrow.

He closed his eyes and visualized the final game. Piney Woods, most likely. That's what the tournament pattern suggested. Which meant they needed a new strategy, one that didn't rely on Tony's sniper skills.

An idea formed in his mind. It was risky, and it required perfect coordination. But it might work.

Joey opened his laptop and typed notes. By the time he finished, it was past midnight. But he had a plan.

Now he just had to hope his team could execute it.

Chapter Forty-Five
ST. ANNE'S CEMETERY

Agent Barnes drove through the gate of St. Anne's Cemetery and along the winding road speckled with gravestones across acres of trimmed grass. The cemetery was old, well-maintained, and eerily quiet. Tony sat in the back seat with his father, taking in every detail of the landscape.

Barnes drove until he got near the back of the cemetery, where the road ended in a small circular turnaround. "This is the only way back to this part of the cemetery, which is where the ceremony will be."

Renfro pointed to an empty grave on the left as Barnes parked the car. It sat about a hundred feet from the road, surrounded by other graves in various states of age and upkeep. "The president will be near the back, by the burial site."

Tony looked around as they exited the car. The air was cool despite the afternoon sun. A light breeze rustled the leaves of the massive oaks that dotted the cemetery. It was peaceful, beautiful even. And potentially deadly.

"We should check all the gravestones big enough to hide a man," Tony said.

Barnes nodded, his expression neutral. "Of course. Anything else?"

"You have binoculars?"

Renfro handed him a pair without comment. Tony raised them and scanned the cemetery from east to west and back again. He picked out potential shooting positions, cover points, and escape routes. He'd done this thousands of times in the game. The real world wasn't much different.

He pointed to a large oak tree near the back, about thirty yards in front of a wrought-iron fence that surrounded the cemetery. "That tree is a logical place for them to plant a sniper."

He focused the binoculars on a spot in the tree where numerous branches went off in different directions, creating a natural platform. "See that crook in the tree? A person could sit there and not be noticed."

Barnes crossed his arms. "I checked that myself."

Tony lowered the binoculars and looked at the agent. "I'd put two agents to guard it anyway. Cover all the bases. The new GPS apps on a phone are so accurate they can read that crook in the tree, and drop someone in place."

He continued scanning, his head moving in smooth, methodical sweeps. Then he pointed to a tree to the west, this one closer to the road. "Put a few men on that one too."

Renfro nudged Barnes and smiled. "Pretty sharp, kid."

Tony smiled back, unfazed. He scanned the area again, then stopped abruptly. "See those three graves near the rear? They're perfect locations."

Barnes followed Tony's pointing finger. "They were digging them for burials, but we had to stop them. Cemetery management wasn't happy about it."

Tony looked up at Barnes, his expression serious. "Can we see them?"

Barnes exchanged a glance with Renfro, then shrugged. "Sure. Why not?"

All of them headed toward the gravesites Tony had mentioned. They walked in silence, their shoes crunching on the gravel path. The open graves loomed ahead, dark rectangles cut into the earth.

"How does an open grave pose a threat?" Barnes asked as they approached.

Tony stopped at the edge of the first grave and looked down into it. Six feet deep, walls of dark earth, a pile of dirt beside it covered with a tarp. "I know you guys don't buy into my theory, but imagine that these terrorists can do what I said — teleport using GPS coordinates."

He turned to face the agents. "If they can do that, they could have gotten the GPS coordinates beforehand. Hell, they could even have had the guys who dug the graves get them. All that's left is to teleport to the grave, pop up, and take a shot."

Barnes opened his mouth to object, but Tony continued before he could speak.

"That's why I mentioned the gravestones and the trees. I wasn't expecting you to find a person. All they need is to have a game system planted there, or close to there."

Tony pointed to a large gravestone next to a tree, maybe forty feet from where they stood. The stone was ornate, carved granite with an angel on top. "See that gravestone? They could plant a game system anywhere that's close — say, I don't know, Bluetooth close — fifty yards or so if it's a new system. And the terrorist could pop up anywhere within fifty yards of that."

Barnes smirked, and Tony could see the agent was trying to be patient but clearly thought this was a waste of time. "Even if they could do that, I doubt they'd try. We've got all escape plans covered."

Tony shook his head and laughed, but there was no humor in it. "They don't need escape plans. If they have a system, five seconds after they shoot, they'll be halfway around the world, and there won't be anything you can do. I heard you experienced that already — with the decoy?"

He let that sink in for a moment, then added, "If you do this your way, the president will be dead."

Barnes pulled Renfro aside and whispered, but Tony's hearing was sharp. "Who the hell does this kid think he is?"

Sean, who'd been hanging back, paused mid-step. His ears tuned in to the conversation. He moved closer, then stepped forward, placing himself between the agents and his son.

"If I were you, I'd listen to him," Sean said quietly. "Tony may seem detached, even awkward at times, but that's because he's autistic."

Barnes' eyes widened, his mouth slightly agape. His breath caught as he leaned forward and stared. The word seemed to shift something in his perception.

Sean continued, his voice steady and proud. "Last year he memorized the flight patterns of every bird that visited our backyard, and he catalogued them by species, time of day, wind conditions, and more. To this day, he can tell me when the Purple Martins, the tanagers, or the warblers will pass by, and he's never been wrong."

Barnes seemed to struggle with how to respond. Finally, he said, "So I guess you want us to take his advice?"

Sean didn't hesitate. "Agent Barnes, for all the problems he has, he's also blessed." He paused. "He can recall every move the terrorist team has made in the past month — probably longer. He knows what weapons they use and when they use them. He not only understands their tactics — he predicts them."

Sean put his hand on Tony's shoulder. "If it were me, I'd want him on my team."

Barnes exchanged another glance with Renfro. "We'll think on it, Lugullo."

Tony walked up behind his father. "No you won't. But give me a few minutes and I'll show you why you should."

He placed the game system he'd been carrying on a gravestone. The agents watched him with a mixture of curiosity and skepticism. Tony rejoined the Secret Service team and pulled out his phone. "Brie, are you near a system?" Tony asked when she answered.

"Yeah, why?" Her voice came through clearly.

"I'm going to text you GPS coordinates. I want you to get to the shack and teleport here." He paused. "Okay, sending them now."

Tony quickly typed the coordinates and sent them. Then he looked at Barnes and Renfro. "Remember when I told you they could get here and disappear? Wait a few minutes, and I'll show you how."

A heavy silence lingered. Barnes exhaled, glancing at Renfro, uncertainty flickering in his eyes. They stood in the cemetery, the wind picking up slightly, rustling leaves and making the tarp over the dirt pile flap gently.

Barnes checked his watch several times. Two minutes passed. Three. Four. He was about to speak when —

Brie appeared.

One moment the space a few feet from them was empty. The next, there was a shimmer in the air, a brief distortion like heat waves, and Brie materialized right in front of them.

"What do you need?" she asked Tony, as casually as if she'd just walked up.

Renfro's mouth fell open. He turned to Barnes, who looked like he'd seen a ghost. "I say we go with what he says."

Barnes turned his back and walked in a small circle, his hand running through his hair. He was processing what he'd just witnessed, and it clearly shook him to his core. When he returned to Tony and Brie, his expression had changed. The skepticism was gone, replaced by something like fear.

"What do you suggest?" Barnes asked.

Tony remained quiet for a moment while he studied the area again. He walked to the edge of one of the open graves and looked down, then at the surrounding terrain. He was calculating angles, distances, sight lines.

"I'd put snipers to guard each of the trees," he said. "If anyone suddenly appears, shoot him. But more importantly, I'd have half a dozen men watching those empty graves — two for each. That's where I think they'll attack from."

He turned to face the agents. "But make sure they aren't noticeable. Position them where they can watch the graves, but they can't be easily spotted."

Renfro nodded eagerly. "We'll put six men guarding each plot."

Tony shook his head firmly. "You don't want that. They'll be watching for sure, and if they see a lot of men guarding those open graves, they'll simply move on and go after the president another day." He paused. "We want to stop them, so let them think they have a shot."

Barnes ran his hand over his face, the weight of responsibility settling on him. "As much as I don't like saying it, your plan sounds good."

"Sir," Tony said, "if you're fond of our president, I suggest you allow me and my team to be here to help."

Barnes laughed, but it was more from stress than humor. "You're goddamn crazy."

"Barnes, this is the president," Renfro said quietly.

Renfro turned to Tony, his expression serious. "There's no way we can let you help. If anything happens to you, to any of you kids —"

Sean pulled Tony aside and moved next to the agents, his voice low but firm. "I don't want him exposed to danger."

"Dad —"

"No," Sean said. "I brought you here to consult, not to fight terrorists."

Tony met his father's eyes. "And what happens when they don't listen? When they miss something because they don't understand how WolfDen thinks?"

"That's their problem, not yours."

"It'll be the president's problem," Tony said quietly. "And a lot of other people's."

Sean looked at his son for a long moment. This kid who could barely keep track of his homework, who struggled with social situations, who needed reminders to shower — this same kid was standing in a cemetery telling Secret Service agents how to protect the president. And he was right. Sean knew he was right.

"We'll see," Sean said.

Brie, who'd been watching the exchange, spoke up. "Mr. Lugullo, if it helps, we're already targets. They tried to burn down your house. We're in this whether we like it or not and our best chance to be safe is to stop them here."

Sean nodded, and Barnes looked at all of them — Tony with his analytical stare, Brie with her calm confidence, Sean with his protective stance. He sighed heavily.

"Let me talk to my superiors," Barnes said. "No promises. But I'll make the case."

"That's all I'm asking," Tony said.

After Barnes and Renfro walked away to make calls, Sean turned to Tony. "You did good, son."

"Did I convince them?"

"I think so. That teleportation deal with Brie sealed it."

Tony looked back at the open graves. "I hope it's enough. Because if they attack the way I think they will, we're going to need every advantage we can get."

Brie moved to stand beside him. "You really think they'll go for the graves?"

"It's what I'd do," Tony said. "Maximum surprise, clear shot, instant escape. It's the perfect play."

"Then we'll be ready," Brie said.

Tony hoped she was right. Because if they weren't, a lot of people were going to die.

Chapter Forty-Six
THE FINAL STAND

That night in the Marriott hotel, Tony dialed Joey. His hands were shaking slightly as he waited for his brother to pick up.

"Where the hell are you?" Joey's voice came through sharply. "We need you here."

"I'm not gonna be there," Tony said. "And even worse, I'm calling to ask if the team can come to D.C. Brie's already here."

"Are you fucking nuts? The final game is tomorrow."

"I hear you, bro, but the president's life is in danger, and we're the best chance to stop them."

Silence on the other end. Tony could picture Joey pacing, running his hand through his hair the way he always did when stressed.

"Shit, I don't know," Joey said.

"Get the rest of the team, and we'll decide jointly."

Joey hemmed and hawed. Tony waited, knowing his brother was wrestling with this. Tournament versus president. Game versus reality.

"All right," Joey said. "We'll call you back."

"We don't have much time."

Tony hung up and sat on the edge of the hotel bed. Brie was in the room next door with Sean. They'd spent the afternoon going over the cemetery layout, planning positions, discussing contingencies. Now all they could do was wait.

An hour later, Tony's cell phone rang.

"Everybody's here," Joey said. "Even Ritchie."

"Did you fill them in?"

"We've got a mixed view on this. Ritchie's in, but Pete and I have doubts."

Tony closed his eyes. He'd expected this. "Whoever's coming, get to the shack at 9:00 AM and teleport. I'll send coordinates. They're the same ones Brie used."

"Tony —"

"Joey, I need all of you. This is bigger than the tournament."

Another pause. "Fine. We'll be there."

After Tony hung up, he texted the coordinates to Joey, then added: *Don't tell Dad. He doesn't want us here.*

The response came back immediately: *I figured out that much.*

Back at the Lugullo house, Joey gathered the team in his bedroom and explained the situation. Pete sat on the beanbag, arms crossed. Ritchie perched on the edge of the sofa, leaning forward.

"Tony wants us to go to D.C. so we can help save the president," Joey said.

"Like hell," Pete said. "Why risk our lives for him? What's he done for us? He didn't even legalize marijuana, like he promised."

"We've only got one game left," Joey said, though his voice lacked conviction.

"And we've only got one president," Ritchie said quietly.

Joey looked at each of them. Pete scowling, Ritchie earnest, both waiting for him to make the call. This was on him. Whatever happened, he'd be the one who decided.

"Ah, shit," Joey said. "I don't want to, but I guess we'll go to D.C."

Pete stood up. "This is insane."

"Probably," Joey agreed. "But Tony's never been wrong about Wolf-Den. If he says this is real, it's real."

He called Tony and verified the coordinates for the cemetery. "We're coming," Joey said.

"Good. And Joey? This is real, so don't get brave."

"Since when do I get brave?"

"Since you decided to fight terrorists instead of playing video games."

Joey managed a laugh despite his nerves. "Fair point. See you tomorrow."

The next morning at St. Anne's Cemetery, Renfro dropped Tony off fifty yards from the empty gravesites. The cemetery was already filling with mourners, black-clad figures moving among the headstones. Secret Service agents in dark suits and sunglasses had taken up positions surrounding the graves Tony identified.

Tony stood with Barnes, close to where President Hatcher would be standing for the eulogy. The president arrived moments later, flanked by six agents. When he saw Tony, he looked down and smiled.

"What are you doing here?" President Hatcher asked.

"Here to help protect you, sir."

President Hatcher laughed, a genuine sound that seemed out of place given the circumstances. "I feel safer already."

Hatcher turned to Renfro and whispered something Tony couldn't hear. Renfro nodded and walked over to Barnes, pulling him aside.

"The man says we should keep Tony out of harm's way," Renfro said quietly.

Barnes cast a quick glance toward President Hatcher, then back to Renfro. "I've been against his involvement from the beginning, but Tony showed me something." He paused. "No matter what, we need to keep him away from danger."

Renfro smiled grimly. "And keep him away from guns."

"We can do that."

Tony heard all of this but said nothing. He knew they'd try to protect him. He also knew that when the shooting started, all bets were off.

Across town, Cyrus greeted Rizwan and two new members in a safe house. Farouz was thirty, intense and aggressive, with the look of someone who'd seen combat. Azerbi was thirty-five, strategic and logical, his movements precise and calculated.

"Today is the day?" Farouz asked.

"And we have everything ready," Cyrus said. "The gravediggers even left several systems for our escape."

"Lead the way," Azerbi said.

They logged into the game together, their avatars appearing in Urban Sprawl. Cyrus led the WolfDen members through the northern part of the territory at a fast pace. They moved quickly through the Piney Woods until they reached the shack.

Cyrus signaled the group to halt. "The building up ahead is our point of interest. We need to be inside for this to work."

Inside the shack, Cyrus and his team entered the GPS coordinates. "Change your clothes before I activate the button," Cyrus said. "The rest of you teleport using the other coordinates. You will reappear in a grave, but it has a system inside the coffin."

The team changed into suits and ties, blending in as mourners. Milliseconds later, they appeared in St. Anne's cemetery — some behind a large marble mausoleum, the others inside the open graves, hidden from view.

Cyrus prepared his weapon to fire. He hugged the back side of the mausoleum to remain unseen. The stone was cold against his back. He could hear the eulogy beginning, the president's voice carrying across the cemetery through speakers.

Farouz lay on the ground behind another marker and scanned the area. He spotted Secret Service agents positioned around the gravesite, but their attention was focused outward, watching for conventional threats. They weren't looking at the graves themselves.

"He's about to speak," Farouz whispered through his comm.

"In ten seconds, we pop out and shoot," Cyrus said. "Once he's down, use the systems to escape."

At that moment, Joey and the GhostWalkers team appeared at the coordinates Tony had given them. The teleport system was hidden in a car parked nearby. The shimmer of their arrival was brief, barely noticeable.

Brie immediately paced behind the president's position, scanning for threats. Joey and Ritchie made their way toward the trees Tony had identified. Pete wandered south among the gravestones, searching places the Secret Service agents might have missed.

Renfro spotted them and his face went red. "Get those fuckin' kids out of here!"

But there was no time.

As Pete rounded the corner of a hedge, he saw one of the WolfDen members hiding behind a large gravestone marker. His eyes went wide. He signaled frantically to an agent who came running.

The agent dropped to one knee beside Pete, aimed, and fired. The shot hit Azerbi in the chest. Kill shot. The terrorist dropped without a sound.

All hell broke loose.

Brie reacted immediately, rushing toward the president, but Barnes was closer. He tackled President Hatcher to the ground, covering him with his body.

Renfro fired on the other WolfDen members, his shots precise and controlled. One bullet caught Rizwan in the arm. The terrorist stumbled but didn't go down.

Farouz returned fire, his bullet passing so close to Renfro's head that the agent felt the displacement of air. Renfro dove for cover behind a headstone. Farouz then took out another agent, dropping him with one shot to the chest.

Cyrus, still hidden behind the mausoleum, stepped out and fired at Pete. The bullet hit Pete in the neck. Blood sprayed. Pete's hands went to his throat, his eyes shocked and disbelieving. He fell to the ground, flopped a few times like a landed fish, then lay still, blood pooling on the grass beneath him.

"Pete!" Tony screamed.

"No!" Ritchie ran toward his friend.

Brie grabbed Barnes' backup gun from his ankle holster and tossed it to Tony. He caught it instinctively, his hands remembering the weight and balance of a weapon even though this was real, and not a game.

He crawled across the ground and positioned himself to get a clear shot at Cyrus. His mind went into the calm, analytical space he inhabited when sniping. Wind — minimal, maybe three miles per hour from the east. Distance — approximately eighty yards. Target moving — no, stationary behind cover. He waited for Cyrus to show himself.

Cyrus poked his head out, searching for the president. Tony focused and fired three times. All three shots hit Cyrus. Two were kill shots — one to the chest, one to the head. The terrorist leader went down hard and didn't move.

Renfro and two other agents tracked the remaining WolfDen members who were coming in from different sides. When they were close enough, Renfro opened fire. His first shot finished off Rizwan, who'd been trying to flee despite his wounded arm. The other agents hit Farouz with two kill shots. He collapsed between headstones, his blood staining the white marble.

The shooting stopped as suddenly as it had started. The cemetery fell silent except for the ringing in everyone's ears and someone screaming in the distance.

Joey and Brie checked the area one more time, making sure there were no other threats, then they joined Tony and Ritchie, who were kneeling over Pete's body.

Joey got on his knees and wrapped his arms around Pete, not caring about the blood that soaked into his clothes. "Son of a bitch. Son of a bitch! Look what they did to Pete."

Pete choked on his blood, but managed a few words. "Ritchie, tell my dad I helped save the president."

Ritchie wiped tears from his eyes and leaned over Pete. He pressed both hands on the wound in Pete's neck, trying desperately to stop the bleeding. "You're gonna be able to tell him yourself. Help's coming."

Pete reached for him, but his arm dropped halfway. The light in his eyes dimmed.

"No," Ritchie said. "Not you, Pete. Not you!"

Tony and Brie stood behind Joey and Ritchie, somber expressions on their faces. Brie was crying, tears running down her cheeks. Tony's face was blank, shock settling in.

Barnes appeared behind them, his weapon still drawn. He holstered it and patted Joey on the back, then rubbed his hair in an awkward gesture of comfort.

"Come on, son," Barnes said gently. "We'll get him taken care of and get him home. In the meantime, how about you and your team go with Renfro so he can get you on the plane."

Ritchie rushed over and hugged Tony and Joey. He held them tightly and kissed their heads while holding back tears. They were still kids, Barnes realized. Just kids who'd somehow ended up in the middle of an assassination attempt.

Sean appeared, running across the cemetery. When he saw his sons covered in blood, kneeling over Pete's body, his face went white. "Jesus Christ, what are you doing here? I told you not to come."

He pulled them to him and hugged them fiercely. "I'm sorry, boys. I'm so sorry."

Secret Service men rushed past, ushering President Hatcher to his limousine. The president was shaken but unharmed, thanks to Barnes' quick action.

"The plane is waiting," Sean said. "Time to go."

But before they left, Sean rushed over to speak to the president. One of the Secret Service men moved in front of him, holding up his hand, but President Hatcher intervened.

"Let him through," Hatcher said.

Sean approached, and the president shook his hand firmly. "Thank you, Agent Lugullo. Your sons are heroes. All of them."

"They're just kids, sir."

"Kids who saved my life." Hatcher looked over at the team. "And don't worry, we're going to shut that gaming company down for good."

Hours later, on the United Airlines flight back to Houston, Tony and Ritchie sat in seats 2A and 2B. Joey and Brie sat behind them. The plane was quiet, most passengers reading or sleeping, unaware that the kids in rows two and three had just stopped an assassination.

Brie rested her head on Joey's shoulder and fell asleep almost immediately. The adrenaline crash had hit her hard. Joey leaned against her, and despite everything, he soon fell asleep as well.

"What are you thinking about, Ritchie?" Tony asked. "You're staring at nothing."

"Just thinking about Pete. I can't believe he's gone."

"I thought you didn't like Pete."

A tear ran down Ritchie's cheek, and he wiped it away quickly. "No. We argued a lot ... But I liked him. I don't have many friends, but Pete was the best."

Tony patted his arm. "It's all right. Pete was a pain in the ass, but I liked him too." He paused. "The president said he'd help us. Maybe he'll get you into college."

"I don't want to go to college," Ritchie said. "I want Pete back."

Tony didn't know what to say to that, so he said nothing. They sat in silence for a while, the drone of the engines the only sound.

The plane hit a few spots of turbulence and Brie woke up. She looked disoriented for a moment, then remembered where she was. She leaned over and kissed Joey on the lips.

Joey stirred and looked over at her, managing a small smile. "Nice way to wake up."

"We did good, Joey," Brie said quietly. "It was great helping you out."

"It doesn't have to be over. We need a new team member."

Brie smiled sadly and kissed him again. "Yeah. We do."

ACKNOWLEDGMENTS

It is with great honor that I give eternal gratitude to my wife, all four of my grandkids, and my great-grandson. They give me the inspiration to keep going.

ABOUT THE AUTHOR

Giacomo Giammatteo is the author of gritty crime dramas about murder, mystery, and family. He also writes nonfiction books, including the No Mistakes Careers, No Mistakes Publishing, No Mistakes Grammar, and No Mistakes Writing series.

When Giacomo isn't writing, he's helping his wife take care of the animals in their sanctuary. At last count, they had forty-five — eleven dogs, one horse, six cats, and twenty-six pigs.

Oh, and one crazy — and very large — wild boar, who takes walks with Giacomo every day and also happens to be his best buddy.

nomistakespublishing.com
gg@giacomog.com

f X

ALSO BY GIACOMO GIAMMATTEO

And you can buy them on the platform of your choice.

This brings up a thought: With more than eighty books out now, it is becoming difficult to try to update the list at the back of all of them. If you want to know what books I have out, use the link above, which takes you to my website, or download the latest copy of my GG recommended reading list, which is free.

Nonfiction

Careers

No Mistakes Resumes, Book I of No Mistakes Careers

No Mistakes Interviews, Book II of No Mistakes Careers

Grammar

Misused Words, No Mistakes Grammar, Volume I

Misused Words for Business, No Mistakes Grammar, Volume II

More Misused Words, No Mistakes Grammar, Volume III

Visual Grammar (This is a compilation of volumes I–III with a bit of new information added. It also includes pictures and is the world's first visual grammar book)

Misused Words and Then Some, No Mistakes Grammar, Volume V

Simply Put: The Plain English Grammar Guide

How to Capitalize Anything

More Grammar

No Mistakes Grammar Bites, Volume I: Lie, Lay, Laid, and It's and Its

No Mistakes Grammar Bites, Volume II: Good and Well, and Then and Than

No Mistakes Grammar Bites, Volume III: That, Which, and Who, and There Is and There Are

No Mistakes Grammar Bites, Volume IV: Affect and Effect, and Accept and Except

No Mistakes Grammar Bites, Volume V: You're and Your, and They're, There, and Their

No Mistakes Grammar Bites, Volume VI: Passed and Past, and Into, In to and In

No Mistakes Grammar Bites, Volume VII: Farther and Further, and Onto, On, and On To

No Mistakes Grammar Bites, Volume VIII: Anxious and Eager, and Different From and Different Than

No Mistakes Grammar Bites, Volume IX, A While and Awhile, and Envy and Jealousy

No Mistakes Grammar Bites, Volume X, Could've and Should've, and Irony and Coincidence

No Mistakes Grammar Bites, Volume XI: "Quotation Marks and How to Punctuate Them" and "Plurals of Compound Nouns"

No Mistakes Grammar Bites, Volume XII: "Latin Abbreviations"

No Mistakes Grammar Bites, Volume XIII: "Redundancies" and "Ax to Grind"

No Mistakes Grammar Bites Volume XIV: "Superlatives and How We Use them Wrong"

No Mistakes Grammar Bites Volume XV: "Shoo-in and Shoe-in" and "Horse Racing Sayings"

No Mistakes Grammar Bites Volume XVI: "Which and What" and "Since and Because"

No Mistakes Grammar Bites Volume XVII: "Hyphens, and When to Use Them" and "Em Dashes and En Dashes"

No Mistakes Grammar Bites Volume XVIII: "Words Difficult to Pronounce" and "Could Not Care Less"

No Mistakes Grammar Bites Volume XIX, "Punctuation" and "When You Don't Need the Word Personal"

No Mistakes Grammar Bites, Volume XX, "When Is Currently Needed?" And "Intervene and Interfere"

No Mistakes Grammar Bites, Volume XXI: "More Hyphen Questions" and Myself, Me, Themselves and Themselves."

No Mistakes Grammar Bites, Volume XXII: "Words You May Be Using Wrong, Part One"

No Mistakes Grammar Bites, Volume XXIII: "Words You May Be Using Wong, Part II"

No Mistakes Grammar Bites, Volume XXIV: "If and Whether," and "Incredible"

No Mistakes Grammar Bites, Volume XXV: "Use or Utilize" and "Dilemma"

No Mistakes Grammar Bites, Volume XXVI: "Alternate and Alternative" and "Plethora"

Writing

No Mistakes Writing, Volume I: Writing Shortcuts

No Mistakes Writing, Volume II: How to Write a Bestseller

No Mistakes Writing, Volume III: Editing Made Easy

No Mistakes Writing, Volume IV: Writing Rules for Writers Who Don't Like Rules
(coming soon)

Publishing

How to Publish an eBook, No Mistakes Publishing, Volume I

How to Format an eBook, No Mistakes Publishing, Volume II

eBook Distribution, No Mistakes Publishing, Volume III

Print on Demand—Who to Use to Print Your Books, No Mistakes Publishing, Volume IV

Other Nonfiction

Uneducated

Whiskers and Bear, Volume I, Sanctuary Tales

A Collection of Animal Stories, Volume II, Sanctuary Tales

More Animal Stories, Volume III, Sanctuary Tales

Surviving a Stroke—Or Two

Life and Then Some

Fiction

Friendship & Honor Series

Murder Takes Time

Murder Has Consequences

Murder Takes Patience

Murder Is Invisible

Murder Is a Promise

Murder Is Immaculate (coming soon)

Blood Flows South Series

A Bullet for Carlos: A Connie Gianelli Mystery

Finding Family, a Novella

A Bullet from Dominic

The Good Book

The Ranger

Redemption Series

Necessary Decisions: A Gino Cataldi Mystery

Old Wounds

Promises Kept, the Story of Number Two

Premeditated

The Ranger

Rules of Vengeance Series (Fantasy)

Light of Lights (the beginning, a novella)

A Promise of Vengeance

Undeniable Vengeance

Consummate Vengeance

Vengeance Is Mine (2019)

Note: *Light of Lights* is a novella. It's about 100 pages long and sets the stage for the series. The other books in the series are between 650 and 850 pages long.

Other Books

You can always see current and upcoming books on my website.

Fiction

Memories for Sale (mystery/sf)

The Joshua Citadel (SF novella)

Children's Books

No Mistakes Grammar for Kids, Volume I: Much and Many

No Mistakes Grammar for Kids, Volume II: Lie and Lay

No Mistakes Grammar for Kids, Volume III: Bring and Take

No Mistakes Grammar for Kids, Volume IV: "Would've, Should've" and "Your and You're"

No Mistakes Grammar for Kids, Volume V: "There, They're, and Their" and "To, Too, and Two"

Shinobi Goes to School—Life on the Farm for Kids, Volume I

Fiona Gets Caught, Life on the Farm for Kids, Volume II

Coco Gets a Donut, Life on the Farm for Kids, Volume III

Squeak Gets a Home, Life on the Farm for Kids, Volume IV

Biscotti Saves Punch, Life on the Farm for Kids, Volume V

The Adventures of Adalina, Volume I: Adalina and the Five Tiny Bears

Coming Soon

The Adventures of Adalina, Volume II: Adalina and the Underwater Bears

Get on the mailing list, and you'll be notified of release dates and sales.

www.ingramcontent.com/pod-product-compliance
Lightning Source LLC
LaVergne TN
LVHW012041070526
838202LV00056B/5550